Infliction

Mech Wars Book 4

Scott Bartlett

Mirth Publishing
St. John's

INFLICTION

© Scott Bartlett 2017

Cover art by: Tom Edwards (tomedwardsdesign.com)

This novel is a work of fiction. All of the characters, places, and events are fictitious. Any resemblance to actual persons living or dead, locales, businesses, or events is entirely coincidental.

Library and Archives Canada Cataloguing in Publication

Bartlett, Scott

Infliction / Scott Bartlett ; illustrations by Tom Edwards.

ISBN 978-1-988380-10-0

To my sister, Danielle.

CHAPTER 1

Live by the Ledger

"The Progenitors have not kept up their end of the deal," said Suzanne Defleur, sweeping silver hair from her eyes. Defleur was chairperson of the Darkstream board, and she had a regal air even in normal life, but in the medieval fantasy that lucid had concocted for the Darkstream board meeting her deep purple robes only heightened the effect.

Before answering, Bob Bronson squinted closer at those robes. *Is that...Quatro fur?* It certainly resembled garments he'd seen made from Quatro coats, and he would have put money on Defleur owning such a garment in real life.

"On the contrary," Bronson said at last, shifting his weight in the chair the sim had provided him. The six board members all sat in thrones, evenly spaced along the back wall of the simulated throne room, and while the chair they'd given him was sumptuous, it was far from throne-like. "The Progenitors have observed our deal to the letter. They promised growth and security for Darkstream's economic prospects, to be achieved via a measured destabilization. That's exactly what we've seen."

"Nothing about the Battle of Vanguard was *measured*," Zane Harris spat. "It was almost a disaster, and if it wasn't for Price showing up in an alien mech, it would have been."

Slowly, Bronson shook his head. "With respect, I think you're discounting the Progenitors' subtlety. Remember who *built* the alien mechs, after all! It's possible they anticipated Price's arrival—engineered it, even. I'm sure they knew the battle would end with Darkstream's losses falling within an acceptable range."

Defleur rearranged her robes around her legs, pulling them tighter. The throne room was a bit drafty, which Bronson had to assume was meant to lend the sim authenticity, though personally he was fine sacrificing some authenticity for comfort. The chill crept inside him, though he knew better than to let on that it was affecting his composure.

Those windows don't even have glass, Bronson thought, his gaze flitting to the row of narrow apertures above the six thrones.

"You speak of possibilities," Defleur said when she'd arranged the showy garment to her satisfaction. "You say you are 'sure.' But I always make a point of reading between the lines, Captain Bronson, and what I'm coming to understand is that the Progenitors have refrained from sharing their methods even with you."

Nodding, Bronson said, "I'll admit, the Progenitors are tight-lipped about a lot of things. But that's exactly how we'd act during talks with a foreign power. Indeed, it's exactly how we *are* acting. I know it's hard to watch the chaos that's gripping

Eresos, but what other method is there for expanding profits so quickly? The war with the Quatro achieved a steady rate of growth, certainly, but we all know how finicky our Steele System shareholders are. Things aren't like they were back in the Milky Way, where we could count on market dominance. The only way to give our shareholders the sort of growth that makes them feel safe is to make sure everyone on Eresos equates Darkstream with safety. We need them howling for contracts with us, and we need them willing to part with limbs to get them. Until everyone on Eresos feels unsafe unless they're huddled against us, we won't have exploited the potential this market has to offer."

"Even so," Harris said. The man spoke little, and when he did, something about the way his voice creaked made others pay attention. "What's our endgame? We cannot very well let our charges die. We do need our customers to continue *living* if they're to continue paying. What happens when we've saturated the market on Eresos? There are no new markets, especially given the fall of Hub, which we moved too slowly to exploit."

"Well, I think we can all agree that there's room yet on Eresos to grow. After all, the Progenitors *did* just do us the favor of removing Red Company for us, our only competitor. As for what happens when Eresos is saturated...well, the Progenitors have assured me that they have a solution."

"Again, this talk of assurances and possibilities," Defleur said. "I'm sick of it."

Bronson stood, spreading his hands with his palms facing the board. "Please. Esteemed members of the board. Haven't I done right by you? Aren't I the one who brought you the battle group of UHF warships, including one with a working wormhole generator? Aren't I the one who helped you ensure that the *Javelin* preserved that wormhole capability, by preventing it from ever getting connected to the master control? And didn't I negotiate our transition out of the wartorn Milky Way, before catalyzing the explosive growth we've seen since settling in the Steele System?"

"You have," Defleur conceded.

"Then please, continue to trust that I'll deliver results. The Progenitors have been masterful in their efforts to help us exploit the Steele System to the fullest. Results don't lie. *Growth* doesn't lie. The way forward might look murky, sometimes, but we have to continue to live by the ledger, don't we? What else is there?"

That brought a protracted silence, followed by a gradual leeching away of the tension that had gripped the medieval throne room.

As always, the board of directors yielded to the confidence and logic of Bronson's words. They were a finicky lot, and they liked to pretend to more power than they had, but in the end, they resumed their actual roles: sit there and let Bronson make them richer.

Which he always did. But in doing so, he enriched himself, and increased his influence over not only them, but everyone involved.

Bronson planned to use the Progenitors, just as he used the board. He doubted that would prove easy, but he considered himself up to the task.

And maybe, someday, the Progenitors would yield to his will too.

CHAPTER 2

Full of Empty Words

Jake and Lisa walked alone along the outskirts of River Rock—or at least, as alone as you could get with an alien padding along a few meters behind you, inside of a giant quadruped mech.

Knowing he likely couldn't speak low enough to avoid being overheard by the quad's enhanced hearing, Jake didn't bother to try:

"Can she be trusted, Lisa?" he asked, glancing backward. The alien piloting the mech, who Lisa called Rug, didn't react to his question. She only continued forward, her pace measured, her scarlet eyes glowing in the gloom that had settled over the region.

"I would trust her with my life," Lisa said. "In fact, I wouldn't be here if it wasn't for Rug and the other Quatro. But I've already told you this, Jake. I don't remember ever having to repeat myself to you. Have you slowed down in your old age?"

The joke came accompanied by a slight smile. Jake was only one year older than Lisa—something she'd managed to tease him about since the day they'd met, in grade school.

And she'll probably tease me about it till we're in our sixties, providing we make it that far...

He cleared his throat, shaking his head to clear away that line of thought. "I know I asked it before. It's just that...it seems pretty clear that whoever made the mechs for the Quatro also made the one I pilot now, and the one that Roach piloted. Why would they do that? Since when does anyone hand over advanced tech to alien species for their own good?"

"You think the alien mechs were given in order to hurt us somehow."

"Yeah."

Lisa's grin returned. "Are you sure you should be looking a gift mech in the mouth?"

Unfortunately, her efforts to cheer him weren't working. "The alien mech I pilot...it whispers to me, Lisa. It tempts me to give up parts of myself, in exchange for more power. Look what it did to Roach. He kept giving to his mech, until there wasn't enough left of him to stay sane."

"Do you really think you'll give in to your mech? Knowing what you know?"

Jake hesitated. "No...no, I'm pretty confident I've learned to control it. But I can't say the same for your friend behind us. Has she shown any signs of erratic behavior?"

Lisa took a moment, her head cocking to one side, causing her raven hair to sway. She'd let it down before they'd taken this walk, and it looked great, if Jake was being honest. A hint of lavender managed to reach him through the still, moist air, and he assumed it must be her shampoo.

"She's mourning the loss of her mate. Who, admittedly, *did* act erratically. He helped us before he died, but before then he was responsible for the deaths of many innocent people." Now it was Lisa's turn to glance backward. "Rug...she's sad, but she's still herself. I'd be able to tell if she was different. We've grown quite close." Lisa's head was still twisted around, and now she smiled at the alien, whose enormous head dipped in response.

"Well, I trust your judgment, Lisa," Jake said.

"Good. But even if you didn't, could we really afford not to retain Rug as an ally, as well as everyone else who's willing to fight with us?"

They were approaching the part of River Rock that bordered the Barrens, having almost completed a full circuit of the village. "No," Jake said. "We can't afford to turn anyone away." He sighed. "Darkstream is still as dominant as they ever were— more, if that's possible. Plus, with the planet's robots turning against us, and with Oneiri shattered..." Shaking his head, he said, "We need everyone we can get."

Lisa's head was cocked to the side once more. "You've changed since we were kids, you know."

"I hope I have!" he said, chuckling.

"Seriously. You're more willing to bend, whereas before you'd have sooner snapped in two before compromising on anything. It seems you've managed to actually acquire some wisdom, Jake Price. Somehow."

At last, Jake smiled. *Looks like she did it after all. She lifted my mood.*

"Have you given any thought to what our next steps should be?" he asked.

"Only in the short-term. I need to rejoin with Andy, and see that he's all right with my own eyes."

"So when's the wedding for you two?" Jake asked, teasing. Although, something else underlaid his ribbing—something that had an edge.

Lisa grinned. "Very funny. All I know is, I'd feel better having Andy with me, especially since I have no idea what's going to happen next on this planet."

"Right. Got it." Jake could sense that edge creeping into his voice, and he did his best to suppress it.

"It seems we both agree that we can't fight Darkstream with our current numbers. Andy is staying with a Quatro drift, and I'd predict that they're ready to join an organized effort to oppose the company that's been oppressing them for decades. They might even be able to help us recruit even more Quatro. Who knows, maybe we'll stumble on what our next steps should be once we reach Andy."

"Makes sense to me," Jake said.

They'd reached the abandoned home Lisa was sharing with Tessa Notaras and a couple members of the militia she'd put together before leaving Alex. Jake sensed that their walk was over.

But before she went inside, Lisa said, "There's something else I wanted to ask you about. As you searched Hub for survivors, and helped them onto the ships that brought them here...did you encounter my father?"

Jake's stomach dropped. "No, Lisa," he said, his voice barely a whisper. "I didn't." Gi Sato hadn't even crossed his mind, which made him feel awful. "I'm sorry. I should have personally ensured that he was located."

She bowed her head. "No, Jake. I understand that the exodus from our home was not exactly orderly." Her eyes rose to meet his. "You risked your life, and you saved so many. I'm truly grateful."

But to Jake, it wasn't good enough. "The refugee fleet is still putting together their passenger manifests, but I'm going to contact them and ask that they specifically search the ships for your father. The moment I have word one way or another, you'll know."

With that, Lisa wrapped her arms around him, gripping him tightly—even tighter than she had when they'd first reunited, out on the Barrens.

"Thank you, Jake," she whispered into his ear. "Thank you. Listen—Marco told me about your sister. I just want you to know how sorry I am. I'll never forget how kind Sue Anne was."

He mustered the best smile he could. "Thank you, Lisa. Thank you. It means a lot."

Lisa went inside, and the moment she did, the same profound loneliness returned that had haunted Jake since the Battle of Vanguard. Even though he was surrounded by friends and allies, ever since Sue Anne's sickness had taken her, he'd felt lonelier than he'd known it was possible to feel.

With her gone, the universe felt empty. She hadn't just been his dear sister, she'd also provided his purpose—he'd built his life around getting enough money to save her somehow.

Well, you failed at that. Didn't you?

Despair always came on the heels of the loneliness, and this time was no exception. He had no idea what was happening in the Steele System, but there were times he felt convinced that he was powerless to stop it.

If he couldn't stop Darkstream, couldn't stop the robot killers that seemed intent on tearing apart the system, then that would be his fault, too. It had been his job to maintain security and stability—he still considered it his job. One he was failing at.

He knew, now, how devastating it was to lose a sister. If he lost his mother and father as well, because he wasn't strong enough...

I can't. I can't let it happen.

But the thought seemed full of empty words, and they didn't provide him any comfort.

CHAPTER 3

Engage Every Hostile

Beth and Henrietta strode the grass-covered surface of Eresos in their MIMAS mechs, and the brittle vegetation crackled underneath their broad metal feet.

Between them walked Captain Bob Bronson, childlike in his comparative shortness.

It wasn't actually Bronson, of course—it was his simulacrum, projected into the mech dream via lucid as he spoke to them from the *Javelin*.

"You're welcome to keep your jobs," he told them. "Even after your stopover at River Rock. But don't try to fool me about the purpose of that little detour."

"We were running recon on Jake Price and the other traitors," Henrietta said, her voice flat. "If we hadn't followed them there, you wouldn't have confirmation that he and Marco Gonzalez plan to betray Darkstream. And you wouldn't know about Lisa Sato and Tessa Notaras at the head of a Quatro horde."

Henrietta's words brought a curt nod from the Darkstream captain. "That's a fine answer. I'll even log it as your explanation for failing to follow my order to come immediately to Valhalla after the Battle of Vanguard. But you still haven't fooled me. I know you were entertaining the idea of turning against us. Consider yourselves both on notice. I'll be keeping an eye on you."

Until now, Beth had been letting Henrietta do the talking, but she sensed that Bronson was about to cut the conversation short, and there was something important that the other MIMAS pilot had so far neglected to ask him.

"Can we get an evac, sir?" Beth asked.

"Negative," Bronson said, and the widening of his grin told Beth he'd been anticipating the question with some eagerness.

"Seriously?" Henrietta said. "Why the hell not?"

"Easy, Jin," Bronson said, his evident mirth intact. "You've just been given your jobs back. You should consider yourselves incredibly fortunate. As for an evac, there's no ship available to park in orbit over your location and wait while you rocket up. Your chance to do that was back at Vanguard. Now you'll have to travel to Ingress and take the space elevator."

"Sir..." Beth said, hesitating. She knew that there was no argument she could make to change his mind, and that she was already treading on thin ice. But she couldn't help stating the obvious. "Eresos is in total chaos. It's safe to assume we're surrounded by hostiles right now, and not just the Quatro. There's also the Gatherers to consider, and the Ravagers, plus we still don't know how a MIMAS will fare against an Ambler—"

"Ravagers?" Bronson said. "Where did you come by that term?"

"P-Price, sir," Beth stammered, and Henrietta's mech whipped its head around to stare at her. She felt pretty sure the other pilot was glaring.

"I see." Bronson's grin had melted into an expression that was all business. "Consider your trek back to Ingress a mission to settle down the countryside."

"How are we supposed to do that?" Henrietta asked.

"By engaging every hostile you encounter. Bronson out." With that, the captain disappeared.

Henrietta was still staring at Beth, and now her mech's hands lifted into the air in an exasperated gesture. "You just had to piss him off, didn't you?"

They continued on toward Ingress. It wasn't long before their HUDs, linked into the system net and kept updated by satellite scans of the planet's surface, alerted them to the presence of an Ambler roaming less than a kilometer to the north, on the other side of a tree-covered rise.

Razor will probably want to interpret Bronson's order as favorably as possible, Beth reflected. For that reason, she kept walking north-west, along a trajectory that wouldn't intercept the Ambler's.

"Where are you going?" Henrietta said, extending the bayonets that had earned her the nickname Razor.

"Bronson told us to take out any hostiles we encountered. I didn't figure you'd consider being a kilometer away 'encountering' them."

"You kidding? I'm itching to see how our mechs stack up against Amblers. Besides, after talking to that dick, I need to blow off some steam."

Steam. Hearing Ash Sweeney's nickname made Beth wince inside her mech, and inside the dream, it lent a red tinge to the sky. *I bet Henrietta used that word to goad me.* The other pilot grew testy when she was angry, and she wasn't above taking it out on her teammates.

Except, they weren't teammates anymore, were they? Oneiri Team was shattered, and they were just individual mercenaries working for a company with questionable motives.

She decided that rising to Henrietta's bait wouldn't serve anything. Instead, Beth extended her own bayonets, and the metallic rasp of the blades projecting from her wrists was as satisfying as always.

"Fine. What's the plan?"

They crept over the hill, which was covered in Eresos' unique species of leafless trees, whose branches cascaded downward in waves until they brushed the ground. As they crested the rise, a gap in those trees showed them the Ambler, surrounded by a group of Gatherers—twenty-one of them, according to Beth's HUD.

"You creep closer while I circle around," Henrietta said. "When I give the signal, engage the Ambler, then melt back into the woods. If I'm right, it'll break rank with the Gatherers to chase you. Once it's far enough away, I'll engage the smaller bots, tear them to shreds. Keep your distance from the Ambler till I can close with it from behind. We'll take it out together."

Beth nodded. "I like it." And she did. She was surprised that Henrietta was playing it so safe, actually—that wasn't typically her MO when she was upset.

Maybe Henrietta's changing. She wouldn't have considered it possible, back during MIMAS training on Valhalla. Then again, Eresos had changed all of them, hadn't it?

As Henrietta went back the way they'd come, to follow a wide route around the hill, Beth inched from tree to tree, taking great care not to offer anything for the Ambler's sensors to detect.

We're lucky it didn't pick us up through that gap in the trees. In truth, Beth had no idea how sophisticated the thing's sensors were. No one did. But she suspected that the coming days would give her a stern lesson in the robots' capabilities.

Henrietta appeared beside her in the mech dream, unclad in her MIMAS. "Now, Paste!" she said, using Beth's own nickname, which Ash had given her. Hearing it brought another pang to her heart.

But she refused to let it get in the way of doing her job. Stepping out from behind a particularly large exemplar of Eresos' native tree, she loosed two rockets at the Ambler.

The towering mech turned toward her as the missiles hissed through the air. One went wide, but the other slammed into its hip, causing it to stagger backward briefly before it charged toward Beth with abandon.

She sprinted forward several steps, her metal fingers retracting to rest against her wrists, revealing the twin rotary auto-cannons built into the MIMAS mech's forearms. Both guns blazed, sending forty rounds per second screaming toward her foe.

Abruptly, Beth about-turned and dashed back into the relative safety of the wood.

Her MIMAS had sensors all over its body, however, and she was able to keep an eye on the Ambler as she fled. That came in handy when the enemy mech sent a pair of rockets at her, followed closely by two more.

Given the way the missiles veered in response to Beth's course adjustments, they clearly had onboard guidance systems.

Not a problem. Their plan involved the woods for a reason, and this was far from the first time she'd ever had highly explosive ordnance sent at her.

Weaving through the wood, she timed her turns so that each rocket found a tree as its target—instead of her backside. Within seconds, four trees blazed behind her, and she was far enough through the woods that the Ambler had lost its visual on her. At least, it stopped firing, anyway.

When Beth reached the hilltop where she and Henrietta had scouted the enemy, she risked a glance back through the gap in the trees.

Sure enough, Henrietta was out on the plain, wreaking havoc on the Gatherers flinging themselves at her with abandon.

They were no match for the MIMAS. True to her handle, Henrietta whirled around and around, slicing through each robot before it could touch her.

But the sound of the Ambler crashing through the trees reached Beth, far too close for comfort. She engaged her flamethrowers, igniting the flora between her and her adversary to buy some time. This close to the Barrens, the trees were all standing tinder, waiting to be set ablaze.

Beth didn't hang around to watch the dancing flames. She fled down the hill.

It took more time than she'd anticipated for Henrietta to catch up, which meant more fleeing across Eresos' uneven landscape for Beth. That made her worry about stumbling across even more enemies.

In the end, her fears went unrealized. Beth watched through her rear sensors as Henrietta overtook the Ambler with surprising stealth, given her speed. The MIMAS collided with the alien machine, driving both bayonets into its midsection.

That didn't stop the Ambler, and it turned to confront Henrietta. But Beth had already turned around and detached her heavy machine gun. She proceeded to pelt the Ambler's back with armor-piercing rounds.

That propelled the Ambler into Henrietta, who plunged her bayonets into the mech once more, pushing it off to fire her autocannons straight into its face, or at least what passed for its face.

"Back up!" Beth shouted as she fired a stream of four rockets at the enemy mech.

Henrietta leapt backward several meters, landing just as the missiles connected with the Ambler—all four of them.

It went down, but Beth wasn't about to assume the job was done. Instead, she trained her newest weapon on the mech; her lasers, which Darkstream had only recently discovered how to use inside planetary atmospheres.

Short seconds later, the Ambler burst into flame, followed by an explosion that flung its parts in several directions for dozens of meters.

Intelligently, Henrietta continued to back up. But as she did, her human likeness appeared before Beth.

"Good work," she said, staring up at Beth's MIMAS.

"You too. Do you have that worked out of your system, now, or are we going to have to engage every hostile the satellites notify us of?"

Henrietta shrugged. "Let's take it a little easier, from here on out. Taking down an Ambler makes for a pretty successful afternoon, in my books. Besides, I have a feeling we got lucky, with this one."

I'm just hoping we make it back to Ingress. But Beth decided not to share that sentiment out loud.

CHAPTER 4

Warzone

Lisa had no mech, and except maybe in extreme circumstances, she wasn't about to let one of them carry her.

She knew her refusal to be carried was slowing down their progress, but she considered her dignity worth it.

Besides, our mission isn't terribly urgent.

Lisa, Jake, and Marco were headed to join up with the Quatro drift who'd taken care of Andy while he recovered from the injuries he'd sustained escaping Alex. The idea was to recruit the Quatro caring for him to join the fight against Darkstream, but at the very least, Lisa would collect Andy and Bob O'Toole, so the effort shouldn't be a total wash.

It'll be close to one, though, if the Quatro don't join. She doubted Andy would be well enough to fight, and Bob O'Toole...she wasn't totally sure regaining O'Toole would help or hinder the revolution she seemed to find herself leading.

At least her army was out doing constructive things, under the guidance of Tessa Notaras and Rug. They were following up on rumors of nearby fighting between humans and Quatro, in the hopes of recruiting the aliens.

Even though Lisa's short, human legs were slowing down the mechs, Marco Gonzalez still managed to fall behind every now and then, lost in the task Jake had assigned him.

"How's your progress on breaking those access control locks, Spirit?" Jake asked after Marco started trailing behind for what felt like the hundredth time. The alien mech Jake piloted towered over Marco's. As intimidating as Lisa found the MIMAS models, the shapeshifting mech was much moreso.

Thank goodness there's only one left, and it's on our side. For now. But she didn't like to think about the possibility of Jake turning against them like Gabriel Roach had.

"Uh," Marco said. "It's coming. I should have access within a couple days."

Jake's mech inclined its head without breaking its stride. "Make it one day."

A sigh projected from the amplifiers installed all over Marco's mech. "I still don't see why we can't just leak the MIMAS training sims to the system net. They'd be hacked inside of an hour, then."

Jake grunted, and said, "You really think the public can break digital locks faster than you?"

"Sure. Don't underestimate the power of crowdsourcing. Anyway, hacking isn't my specialty. Being smart doesn't mean I'm an expert at everything."

"No one said you were smart," Jake said with a chuckle. "Anyway, there's no way we're leaking these to the public. Just because we've turned against Darkstream doesn't mean we're going to start leaking military secrets all over the place. We're only going to leak matters of extreme public interest—like the fact that the company was complicit in enslaving everyone on Alex."

Marco shook his mech's head. "I still don't see how it's dangerous to leak the *sims*. People would still need to obtain actual MIMAS mechs to do any harm with those, and that's incredibly unlikely."

"My decision's final, Marco. We're not leaking the sims."

When Lisa had first asked Jake for access to the training sims, he'd been reluctant. Although he seemed committed to fighting Darkstream in theory, he was still struggling with going through the actual motions. He hadn't seen what she had.

Although, Bronson did order him to abandon his family to die.

Either way, he'd needed some convincing.

"Do you really think we're going to get our hands on more mechs?" he'd said.

"I think we have to. The deck is stacked against us, Jake—so high that it's hard to see the top. If we're going to win this war, we need something to even things up. We *need* to obtain some more mechs."

He'd shrugged uncomfortably. "I just don't think it's very likely."

When she'd answered, her voice had been much softer than before. "Well, isn't it a little *more* likely that something bad could happen to you or Marco while you're outside your mechs? We'd need replacement pilots, if that happened."

After a pause, Jake had said, "You're right. My mech is pretty different from a MIMAS, and I wouldn't wish piloting it on you. But you've convinced me. We can't transmit the sims to you without breaking the access controls protecting them—I'll have Marco get started on that right away."

That comment, about how Jake wouldn't wish piloting his mech on her, had robbed Lisa of sleep that night. But what could be done? They couldn't afford for Jake to stop using the alien mech.

Even if we could afford it, I'm not sure that he would *stop.*

An alert from her implant interrupted her reverie, telling her that they were drawing near the location that Andy had transmitted to her.

The Quatro had learned not to engage in any large troop displacements unless they had an underground tunnel or cave that they knew they could viably retreat too. Aboveground, their superconducting fullerene-laced brains only had enough power to pull the triggers on the artillery they'd acquired, but belowground was a different matter altogether. There, it was cold enough that their ability allowed them to halt bullets before they reached their targets.

Luckily for the Quatro, the topology of Eresos was riddled with such underground hideaways.

If Andy hadn't told her how to find the entrance to this Quatro drift's current lair, she doubted she would have found it on her own, even given the coordinates. Two trees twisted together to huddle up against a hillside, and the gap was such that the Quatro themselves likely had to squeeze through. Lisa had seen several Quatro big enough that she wasn't sure they would have fit at all, though maybe the trees had more give than they appeared to.

Or maybe Quatro are more flexible than I think.

"How are we doing this?" Jake asked. "The mechs aren't getting through there. Not unless we widen the hole, and I doubt your friends would appreciate that."

"It's up to you," Lisa answered. "But like you said, if you come, your mech stays out here."

Jake nodded. "Marco, you keep watch. Drop the hacking for now, okay? I don't want you distracted enough that you let a Darkstream battalion drop on our heads without warning."

"I wasn't *that* distracted!" Marco protested.

"Trust me, Marco," Jake said as the front of his mech opened up to let him leave. "Give the hacking a break."

The temperature dropped with surprising rapidity as Lisa and Jake progressed along the tunnel, and they hadn't gone very far before their weapons were snatched out of their hands to fly into the darkness.

They'd been expecting this, and they both raised their empty hands into the air.

The invisible force gripped the metal in their jumpsuits and walked them gently but firmly deeper down the passage.

Without Rug, they had no means of speaking to the Quatro escorting them, but luckily, Rug had persuaded a member of her drift to leave a translator behind, to facilitate communication between Andy, Bob O'Toole, and the Quatro.

Within minutes, they entered a modest cavern lit by two campfires, filled with Quatro, who Lisa's implant instantly tallied up: "SIXTEEN QUATRO PRESENT."

One of the aliens stepped forward, lowering its enormous head while bending its forelegs slightly, which Lisa knew was a gesture of respect. Metal glinted from around the quadruped's neck—the translator.

The Quatro escorting Lisa and Jake rumbled briefly in the aliens' language, and then the one wearing the translator spoke.

"Welcome, Lisa Sato," the Quatro purred. "I apologize for the precautions, however I have trained my soldiers to treat all humans with wariness, especially humans who make their way into our base. This one is not known to us." The Quatro indicated Jake with its gaze.

"This is Jake Price," Lisa said, "a former Darkstream mech pilot. That is, he still pilots a mech—just not for Darkstream. He's on our side, now. He's a friend."

The alien shifted its gaze to the Quatro holding them and spoke in their tongue. With that, their escort released them from its invisible grasp.

"Thank you," Lisa said.

"You will no doubt wish to see your friends," their host answered. "Follow."

The Quatro turned with more grace than should have been possible, given its size, though Lisa was accustomed to that by now. Even so, when its paws landed, it sent a slight tremor through the rock.

Lisa exchanged brief glances with Jake, to make sure he was taking everything in stride. But her friend had acquired what seemed to be an unshakable calm since they'd last been together several years ago, and unsurprisingly, he appeared collected now.

They passed through a smaller rock chamber into an even smaller one. There, Lisa's eyes fell on Andy, playing chess with Bob O'Toole on a board their implants overlaid on the rock. Andy's eyes met hers, and she sprinted toward him.

"Easy!" he said, using his crutches to struggle to a standing position, and she slowed, embracing him gently.

"I'm just so glad to see you're okay," she said, her head pressed against his chest.

"Thanks," he said. "Although, you left me with only O'Toole for company, in terms of humans. I'm pretty sure my sanity went away a few days ago."

"You could have done a lot worse," O'Toole said from his sitting position.

I'm not sure how, Lisa reflected, though she didn't share the thought. She drew back from Andy, trying not to look at his left leg, which he'd lost below the knee.

"Who's this?" Andy said, and Lisa saw that his gaze had drifted past her to lock onto Jack's. Andy's expression had gone cold.

"Seaman Jake Price," Jake said, stepping forward and offering his hand.

Andy ignored it. "My hands are kind of full," he said, lifting the crutches slightly.

"Apologies," Jake said, lowering his hand briskly.

Lisa felt the corner of her mouth quirk downward. She felt quite sure Andy could have managed to shake Jake's hand, and she wasn't sure why he wouldn't. *Seems a bit petty.*

"Jake is a childhood friend," Lisa said, in an attempt to disarm Andy. "He's from Hub, too."

"I see."

An awkward silence stretched on until, at last, Lisa said, "Well, we'd better get back to the Quatro. We're here to recruit them, too, and if they're willing to join then we need to start planning our next moves."

"Sure thing," Andy said curtly, even though he addressed her, now. "You two go do that. I'll stay here and keep O'Toole occupied."

As she and Jake walked back to the central chamber, Lisa apologized to her childhood friend. "Andy's not usually like that. I guess being in a warzone with half a leg missing has brought him a lot of stress."

She'd meant it as a joke, but it came out a lot darker than she'd meant—and a lot realer.

"Don't worry about it," Jake said. "We're all under a lot of stress."

CHAPTER 5

Window into Your Skull

Ash was visiting Northshire for the first time in years. Her father greeted her at the door, with his booming laugh that seemed to echo off the hills surrounding the town. Then came Jess, her best friend and confidant since...well, since she'd been born.

"*Ash!*" her sister squealed, running out to sweep her into a tight embrace. Pulling back with her hands still on Ash's shoulders, Jess said, "I thought you weren't supposed to be back for another year at least!"

"I..." Ash cocked her head to the right. "I'm not. I'm not supposed to be here."

Blood had begun to leak from the edges of Jess's eyes, to stream down her face in tiny rivulets. Her warm smile never left, though, and her grip on Ash's shoulders remained just as firm.

"I've met a man, Ash, and he doesn't know it yet, but we're going to get married. We're going to start a family."

With the word "family," Jess's eyes melted as though super-heated. Melted dollops, they slid down the blood and fell from her cheeks and onto the ground. The rest of her face was unaffected.

Ash woke from the nightmare, panic seizing her chest and making her heart race.

Her surroundings did nothing to quell her anxiety. Gunmetal-gray surgical tables. Dully reflective steel walls. Sterile white bedsheets, covering twin rows of beds...

A sick bay. The one on Valhalla. She recognized it from when they were all gathered around Gabriel Roach's comatose form.

Roach. He...killed me.

At least, during that final moment of consciousness, with Roach's dark blade projecting from her chest, she had accepted that she would die.

Yet here she was.

The sick bay entrance opened, and a woman wearing a lab coat the same color as the bedsheets entered, approaching the bed. Ash attempted to sit up, to greet the woman, but pain lanced through her body and she cried out softly.

"Easy," the woman said with a slight Eastern European accent that reminded Ash of Beth. "Your body is not yet recovered, though the iatric nanobots have made good progress on that front." The woman offered her a small smile. "I am Doctor Korhonen. You've been out for a few days, and I've been supervising your recovery during that time."

"Thank you," Ash rasped—the loudest she could manage.

After a perfunctory checkup, Korhonen moved toward the only other patient in the room, a young boy who looked no more than nine.

"Wait," Ash said.

Korhonen turned, raising her eyebrows.

"Gabriel Roach," Ash said. "Is he...what became of him?"

"He is dead." The doctor's lips formed a thin line for an instant, and then she continued toward the boy.

Ash was left alone with her thoughts, which kept returning to the question of whether she could have avoided Roach's betrayal. The man had been abusive toward her before, and yet she'd kept following him, because she hadn't trusted her own ability to lead Oneiri. She'd convinced herself that they needed him. And then he'd nearly killed her.

But there was more to the picture than just her reliance on Roach. They'd both been driven by avenging Jess Sweeney's death. Ash had thought that united them. She'd *felt* it. Yet here she was, recovering from Roach's murderous attack.

What does vengeance even mean anymore? Punishing the Quatro for killing her sister had been her primary motivator for persevering through MIMAS training, when hundreds of others had washed out.

I endured Roach's abuse then, too. I told myself it was for the best.

With the data dump DuGalle had provided her, showing how Darkstream used Red Company to provoke the Quatro into war...

Who had truly killed her sister? The Quatro, or her employer?

Suddenly, she remembered what Captain Bronson had said during the Battle of Vanguard, about his willingness to nuke the entire area if the engagement went south, in order to neutralize the hostile robots.

If he was willing to bomb his subordinates from orbit just because they were defeated, robbing them of any chance to retreat...

If Bronson was willing to do that, then he would definitely be willing to bombard any region containing those who'd turned against him. That made her wonder where the rest of Oneiri had ended up. Ash had shared the revelations from DuGalle's data dump with them just before the battle.

She found that her implant still functioned, and so she used it to contact Beth Arkanian.

"Ash," her friend said breathlessly, her sapphire eyes wide. "You're awake!"

"I am. I don't know how, but...I'm awake. I'm alive."

"I, um, I may have had something to do with that. I carried you to a hilltop and I fended off hostiles to keep you safe. Marco helped too, and Jake."

"*Jake?* He's back?"

Beth cast her eyes downward, then. "He is, but...he's gone rogue, Ash. He pilots an alien mech now, and he went rogue, just like Roach did."

Her heart plummeting, Ash whispered, "Oh, no. He attacked you?"

"Well, no. Not yet. But he and Marco have joined up with Quatro, and they're ignoring Captain Bronson's orders to return to Valhalla. It's pretty clear what they're planning."

"Wait, Marco's with Jake? Then Jake can't be unstable like Roach was. Marco wouldn't have joined him, if he was."

Beth's slim shoulders rose and fell. "All I know is he's joined our enemies. That's all I really need to know. I know he's your friend, but..."

"He's a traitor. Yes. I get it, Beth."

"Are you all right?"

"As all right as I can be, I guess. I'm gonna go, okay?"

Beth's eyes went wide again, and then she checked herself. "Okay. Well, take care, Ash."

"You too."

Terminating the transmission, Ash struggled to steady her breathing. Beth Arkanian was dear to her, which made it even harder to process that she was so willing to turn against Jake, to consider him an enemy. Other than her desire to avenge Jess, Jake had been the only reason Ash had gotten through mech training, and she knew that she had done the same for him. He'd told her as much.

Didn't Beth understand that Jake was dear to Ash, too?

She reached out to Jake via the system net, taking care to double-check the encryption first so that not even Darkstream's spies could decipher the content of their conversation.

At least, I hope they can't. Ash knew they'd installed back doors into the implants—both the devices they sold to the public and those they gave their military personnel. She knew about many of those back doors, but it was possible there were some she didn't.

"Ash," Jake said, and the relief and warmth he put into her name told her he didn't consider *her* to be an enemy.

That's a good start. "Jake. I hear you've gone rogue."

He cocked his head to one side. "I hadn't quite thought of it like that, but 'gone rogue' *does* sound a lot cooler than 'treason.'"

"But you don't really see yourself as a traitor, do you?"

"Depends on your perspective. I'm betraying Darkstream, sure. But only after they betrayed the people they swore they're dedicated to protecting."

Ash nodded. "Do you think Bronson considers you a threat?"

"Of course. In fact, I'm a little insulted that you'd insinuate there's any other possibility. I *do* have a horde of Quatro with me, you know. Not to mention a shiny new alien mech."

"Watch yourself with that thing. I assume you know what it did to Roach?"

"I do. And trust me, I'm well aware of its danger."

"Good." Ash paused. "The reason I asked whether you think Bronson considers you a threat...Jake, he doesn't need much prompting to wipe you out with nukes from orbit."

"Seriously? Bronson's a dick, sure, but irradiating an entire region is kind of next level, isn't—"

"He'll do it. He was even going to do it if we lost the battle at Vanguard."

"Wow. I mean...wow."

"Yeah. You need to get Marco to disable the function that broadcasts your implant's coordinates. That, or cut the things out of your heads."

"I'll go with option A. But still, satellite images will still likely show our location after I join back up with our army. With a force that big, there's going to be signs, even from orbit."

"Yeah, but why help Bronson paint a target on your heads? Besides, there are other reasons to disable Darkstream's window into your skulls. Ever heard of OPSEC?"

Smiling wryly, Jake nodded. "You're right. I'll get Marco started on it, though he's not going to be happy. I already have him cracking the access control on the MIMAS sims."

"You—" Ash shook her head as much as she could manage against the pillow. *I'm not going to comment on that news.* "Just stay safe, Jake."

"You too. And get better. Thanks for the tipoff on how crazy Bronson really is."

"You're pretty crazy yourself, you know," Ash said.

"In all the right ways, though, right?"

"Jury's out on that one." Ash terminated the transmission, then, a smile curling the corners of her lips.

CHAPTER 6

Robot Horde

Rug surged through the woods, and with her passage, mighty trees splintered that once would have given her pause.

Once, she would have cared more about the destruction she wrought. But she'd undergone a change.

A corollary of that change was that she ignored the voice telling her she should wait for the rest of her force before engaging. That, as their leader, she needed to see to her own safety before she saw to theirs—and even before the safety of the drift they were attempting to save today.

Your mate would not have condoned this recklessness.

"Then my mate would have been a hypocrite," Rug muttered as she charged forward, her four metal paws rending the earth. It was her mate's recklessness that had saved Rug, and in the aftermath of his death, during her darkest moments, she felt content to continue that tradition until she finally joined him in death.

The trees thinned and fell away entirely as she emerged from the forest and onto the plain, where her dwindling brethren fought an enemy comprised of assorted metal foes: two Amblers, dozens of Gatherers, and a swarm of Ravagers so thick and numerous that even her suit was having difficult tallying them.

The robotic hostiles had the beleaguered Quatro drift surrounded—at least, they had until now. Though Rug's force hadn't caught up yet, she planned to modify the situation on her own if she could.

Veering to the left, reining in the awesome momentum her quad was capable of, she barreled toward a section of enemy forces that was as far from the pair of Amblers as it was possible to get.

The enemy had barely registered her presence, but that quickly changed when she barreled into them, sending Ravagers and Gatherers hurtling through the air.

Dogged and savage as ever, the Ravagers quickly regrouped, turning their efforts on her, trying to get at her mech to rip it apart. That was a real danger, she knew from experience, and if she allowed them unchallenged access for too long, she was done.

But the dynamic of this battle had changed, and the rate of Quatro deaths had slowed. Almost a third of the enemy had turned to react to her attack, and the robot onslaught began to falter.

That analysis flitted through Rug's brain as her flanks morphed, suddenly bristling with twin batteries of energy cannons, which she used to execute simultaneous broadsides, blowing away the front ranks of metal hostiles.

A couple of Ravagers still managed to make it through, and Rug reared on her hind paws, batting one of them out of the air with a forepaw and causing the robot to disintegrate. The maneuver angled the guns projecting from her left side upward, which more than accounted for the second Ravager.

By then, the rest of her Quatro force was emerging from the forest. Though none of them wielded the power Rug's mech afforded her, their sheer numbers were instantly apparent, and they just kept coming.

Rug had learned that the Meddlers' robots did have a self-preservation mechanism, and they seemed to have performed a quick calculus of their odds of winning this engagement, given the new arrivals.

Those odds were not favorable to them, and the tide of metal attackers shifted instantly to flee across the plain.

Roaring and barking, the Quatro gave chase, including those who had been surrounded. Although witnessing such bravery and valor didn't surprise Rug, it still sent a thrill through her as she chased after the retreating robots, savaging their backsides with gun and tooth and claw.

Yes, the whispers began, and Rug struggled to silence them. As so often happened of late, she failed.

Kill them. Kill them all. Start with your foes and finish with your friends. Oblivion is the kindest end.

Not the most pleasant sentiment, to be sure. Despite her inability to control the soft voices that whispered constantly to her from within the suit, she did not share their indiscriminate desire to exterminate. She wanted to exterminate, surely, but only those who'd taken her mate from her.

As Rug harried the metal devils across the plain, Lisa Sato contacted her, a function that the battle suit enabled. That worried Rug—how useful the suit had turned out to be, and also how seamlessly it integrated with human technology. She bore no illusions about the weapon's origin, and she knew that whatever purpose for which it had been designed, it had not been one born of goodwill.

"Rug," Lisa Sato began. "Jake just heard from Ash Sweeney, who claims that Bronson won't hesitate to bomb us from orbit if we became too big a thorn in his side."

Rug slowed her chase, and her quarry immediately began to lengthen the gap between them. "Is he capable of such a thing?"

"Sweeney thinks so. Either way, it's enough to warrant a meeting of resistance leadership. How have your efforts been going?"

"Well," Rug said. "We have joined five drifts to our cause, two which we joined in the midst of battle." The last drift had been beset by Darkstream soldiers, but the outcome of that battle had been the same as today's.

"Excellent work. The drift here is ready to join us, too. All the more reason to meet and decide what our next steps will be. This is urgent, Rug. I need you to name a second-in-command and then leave immediately to join us."

"It will be done, Lisa Sato."

"Good. Thank you, Rug. I'll send you our coordinates now, along with instructions on how to find this drift's lair. I...I don't think your quad will fit."

"I will find a safe place for it."

Ten minutes saw Rug bounding across the countryside. Unlike when the battle fervor had gripped her, she lamented the effect she knew her passage must be having on the ecosystems of Eresos. This time, she took as much care as possible to spare the planet's flora without sacrificing speed.

It was all she could do. Haste had become a necessity for all who remained on Eresos and wished to survive. If Darkstream remained unchallenged, and the robot horde continued to run amok, it was likely that Eresos would soon be left without any stable ecosystems to speak of.

CHAPTER 7

Far from Stable

"Gonzalez," Jake said, opting for a greater level of formality than he normally would have. "Report on your progress with masking our implants' locations from Darkstream."

Marco pushed himself off of the rock and stepped forward. The resistance leadership was meeting in the main chamber of the smallish cave system. In Jake's view, the drift who'd taken over this place as their temporary sanctuary was overrepresented at the meeting, but he supposed that was their due, given they controlled it. He would have taken advantage of it in their place, too.

Of course, since only one of them had a translator, it did slow things down somewhat. The Quatro with the device, who'd chosen the name Plank for himself, paused frequently to translate for the others, which often sparked what seemed to be an intense debate before Plank was allowed to give an answer to whatever had been said.

"I've just about accomplished it," Marco said. "Though my work on the implants has slowed progress on cracking the MIMAS sims."

It's called prioritizing, Marco. Spirit was brilliant, but sometimes Jake found his inability to grasp basic logistics a bit grating.

"That's fine," Jake said. "The bottom line—"

"Is masking your implants truly necessary?" Plank asked. "I know Darkstream to be monstrous, but would they be willing to jeopardize the other humans living on this planet?"

"They've jeopardized them plenty already, if the Red Company leaks are to be believed," Jake answered. "And I don't see why we wouldn't believe them. Either way, I don't think we should sit on our hands—or, uh, paws—to find out. We need to act."

Rug rose to her feet, looking small to Jake. She was big for a Quatro, which was saying something, but he'd mostly only seen her inside her quad.

"We should not act merely for the sake of acting," Rug said. "We must decide on a clear thrust for our actions. What is our goal?"

"Good question," Jake said, nodding. "We're obviously at war, but with whom? Should we focus our efforts on taking down Darkstream or on trying to save the populace from the robots that have turned against them?"

"Darkstream," Lisa said emphatically.

Rug spoke again. "The fact that the Amblers and Gatherers have turned on both humans and Quatro, paired with the arrival of so many Ravagers—there is only one explanation. The Meddlers have returned."

Lisa's expression was carefully controlled, Jake saw. *She doesn't want to insult her friend, but she disagrees. Pretty strongly, I think.*

"Rug..." Lisa said slowly. "You said the Meddlers would return only when the reservoirs are filled with resources from the Gatherers. We're far from that point, and the Gatherers have stopped harvesting altogether. You said the Meddlers wouldn't come for another year at least."

The Quatro swung its massive head toward Lisa. "Clearly, their schedule has accelerated."

"Rug," Marco said, and Jake had to repress an urge to glare him into silence.

The Quatro turned ponderously toward Spirit.

"You say the Meddlers built the robots. But have you ever actually seen a Meddler?"

"No," Rug said after a brief pause. "However, when we were stranded on Alex, my drift did identify a particular model of robot that we became certain was under direct remote control by the Meddlers. Their avatars, in a sense. We based the conclusion on these robots' behavior, as well as the way their fellows strove to protect them at all costs."

"What did those robots look like?" Marco asked.

"Much taller than Gatherers and Ravagers. Taller than humans, and even some Quatro. They were made of silver and gold plates, all woven together, and they wielded immense strength—greater than that of the Ravagers. They had no native weaponry installed, though often they carried guns, in the manner you humans do."

Marco was nodding, considering Rug's words in silence, which lately Jake preferred to the alternative.

Jake cleared his throat and said, "I have to agree with Lisa that Darkstream should be our primary target. I'm sure we'll end up fighting the robots either way, but given the threat of orbital nukes, Darkstream holds everyone and everything in their sway. They also control the main avenue of ingress and egress from Eresos—the space elevator. Rug, I know you advocate for leaving this star system altogether. I'm not saying I'm on board with that, but it is true that retaking the elevator is the first step toward it. Right now, leaving the system isn't an option for us, but if we take the elevator, the possibility will at least open up."

That didn't end the meeting, which would have been too simple. Instead, they talked for hours more. But nothing new was decided after Jake's words, which, one by one, everyone came around to endorsing.

They would take the fight to Darkstream. As the decision was made, a knot of tension unraveled in Jake's chest, one he hadn't realized was there. A glance at Lisa told him that she felt similarly. They shared a warm smile.

Just as he was leaving the meeting, he received an alert from the refugee fleet, which was in high Eresos orbit, keeping their distance from Valhalla Station.

The message was from Ryan Pichenko, who'd been a councilman back in Comet Four. Jake had put him in charge of compiling comprehensive passenger manifests for the entire refugee fleet, which was no mean feat. The man had proved invaluable, though, and he could delegate with the best of them. He had a crack team working around the clock, who'd already made impressive progress.

"Councilman," Jake said. "How are things in orbit? Is Darkstream still leaving you alone?"

"So far. Apparently they haven't yet added piracy to their repertoire, or harassing defenseless refugees."

It's probably only a matter of time. But Jake chose not to say that. "It's nice to get some good news," he said instead.

"There's more where that came from. One of my subordinates has located Gi Sato. He evacuated Hub along with the others, and he's alive and well."

"That's wonderful," Jake said, and he meant it. "Lisa will be relieved."

Pichenko nodded. "He says he wants to visit her."

That gave Jake pause—a long one, while he weighed the prospect Pichenko had raised. Judging from the man's grave frown, the councilman understood the risk involved.

"Eresos is far from what I'd call stable right now," Jake said at last, speaking slowly. "But I understand the need for families to be together, especially during times like these. As long as Mr. Sato understands the danger of coming here, and as long as there's a shuttle pilot willing to take on the task of transporting him, then I'm fine with it."

Pichenko nodded, his expression unchanged. "I'll pass that along."

CHAPTER 8

Bonds

In the beginning was pain.

Pain, refracted as through a prism.

Pain, reflected back and forth, like light shone through a darkened funhouse.

The pain was multiplied countless times over, not because it grew over time, but because it was experienced simultaneously by countless disparate entities. Those entities shared certain memories in common, though no memory was shared by all of them, and there was little for them to recognize in each other.

Gradually, the entities knitted themselves together, slowly realizing that they weren't truly entities at all. Not in the sense of individual, coherent, conscious beings.

No, the 'entities' were merely fragments of a single entity, which once had been whole. This realization came as that former consciousness stitched itself back together, piece by piece, gradually regaining the ability to recognize itself as a "self" at all.

At last, the puzzle was complete, or at least complete enough that a solution could be glimpsed:

Gabriel Roach.

The words echoed down the empty corridors of that shattered mind. And with the passage of what seemed like eons, they became to take on a semblance of meaning.

After his consciousness had fused itself back together, and he'd begun to regain an identity of sorts, he started working on assembling some sort of chronology.

Conceiving of things using time as a framework ended up helping a lot, and soon he even arrived at a plausible explanation for what was happening to him. The mech had stored his consciousness distributed throughout itself in thousands of encrypted chunks, unrecognizable as anything except when combined and ordered.

It had even restored his nervous system, using raw materials it had stored from a previous battle and secreted throughout itself in a similar manner to his consciousness.

It was not a pleasant realization, and he did not commend the machine for its accomplishment. Instead, he cursed it, and he continued to curse it until he fell silent, having realized where the raw materials had come from that had been used to rebuild his nerves and neurons.

They'd come from his own human victims.

How can I stop myself? It was the first complete thought he'd managed, and it was charged with panic. Several more frenetic thoughts followed, each more desperate than the last. *Can I be stopped at all? I should be dead!*

For a long moment, he wished that he had died.

As part of the final steps of coming back online as a unified consciousness, the alien mech's sensor suite kicked in, and Gabe became aware that he was in a titanium-reinforced room much like the one in which Darkstream had held this alien mech before Gabe had become its pilot and inseparable occupant.

Moreover, he was affixed to a titanium slab big enough to accommodate him, held there by hundreds of super-strong nano-tethers.

The mech dream, which he inhabited permanently since fusing with this monstrosity, told him that his motor abilities had been restored to him. And yet, he was unable to break through his bonds.

The reason why quickly became clear: wires extended from nodes fused to his metal body in several places, which were hooked up to an enormous power cell positioned at the foot of the titanium slab.

The alien mech harvested energy from naturally occurring electrical fields using giant silver coils distributed throughout it. It appeared that the power cell near his feet was being used to extract that power as soon as it was generated.

And so, his question had been answered. It seemed someone had stopped him after all.

The realization flooded him with relief.

CHAPTER 9

Access Controls

W*hat have I gotten myself into?* Lisa reflected as she watched hundreds of Quatro pass by the foot of the hill she'd chosen for her meeting with her father.

Watching the force pass below her reminded her of the moments just before the battle with the machine army that had almost been her end. Except, that battle had begun with an ambush. This time, Lisa and her allies were the aggressors.

Everyone seemed to credit Lisa for putting together the resistance force. She wasn't certain whether that was out of a desire to praise her, or to nudge her into a position of leadership—thereby making her responsible for their success or failure.

Sometimes, it occurred to Lisa that allies often had more options for moving against one than enemies did.

Either way, "her" force consisted of one MIMAS mech, one Quatro quad, one bipedal alien mech, a handful of human soldiers left over from the militia she'd started on Alex, and what was now over one thousand Quatro—all devoted to tearing down Darkstream, starting by breaking their hold on Ingress.

And that force was on the move. They'd left the cave-system home of their newest Quatro recruits, and now they ranged across Eresos' landscape, as quickly as a force this size could move.

As such, there were very few opportunities for true privacy. Even the shuttle currently en route to this barren hilltop would contain its pilot, to whom Jake had given strict orders not to leave his seat, in case a hasty takeoff was needed.

Something glinted high up in the sky, then vanished. Lisa watched that space until the glint reappeared, quickly resolving into a dark-gray dot, which soon became recognizable as a shuttle from the refugee fleet that had fled Hub. It wasn't a combat shuttle, like the old UHF ones that had been brought here from the Milky Way. Those were in short supply, and all under the control of Darkstream.

No, the shuttle carrying her father was newer, and much smaller, allowing it to settle on Lisa's hilltop with room to spare.

Despite Jake's orders, the shuttle pilot did leave his seat—to help Gi Sato out of the airlock. The pilot tipped his cap to Lisa once she held her father's hand, smiled, then disappeared back into his shuttle.

That's the problem with giving civilians orders. Might as well try to uncrack an egg.

Once the pilot was gone, Lisa swept her father into a gentle embrace, shocked at how thin and frail he felt in her arms.

Drawing back, she got her first good luck at him. Deep creases lined Gi Sato's face, and his short hair had turned the color of iron. His arms, once bulging with muscle, had lost much of their mass. His muscles *were* still there, except now they were lean and wiry. Gi Sato was still tall, but now he stooped slightly.

Has it really been so long?

"You are more beautiful than ever," her father said.

Lisa tried to come up with a response born from grace and poise. Instead, she broke into tears, pressing her face against her father's chest. He held her with surprising tightness, given his aged appearance.

"There, there," he said, the tenderness in his voice making her sob harder.

"I can't believe Hub is gone," Lisa choked out. "Your farm...our home..."

"They are dust," Gi Sato said, and his serenity made Lisa pull back to study his face, her tears ceasing as quickly as they'd begun.

"How can you be so calm? We've lost our home! I saw the photos. It's completely ruined." Her father had always been calm, of course, but he'd never had to deal with a catastrophe of this magnitude. Surely losing their home would shake his resolve at least somewhat?

"Any pain except death can be endured," Gi said. "I observe my own pain, and in doing so I learn that it is not my master. You forget, Lisa, that I have lost my home once before. I lost my place in the Milky Way when I fled here."

"But that was no loss. The people there have lost their way."

"And yet, theirs may be the only society left to us now."

Lisa shook her head, wiping her eyes dry with the back of her hand. "What are you saying? We can't return there."

"We must. This is a failed society, here in the Steele System. It must be abandoned."

Lisa drew back farther, struggling not to grimace at her father. This wasn't how she'd pictured their reunion going. "We can make it work, father. We can defeat Darkstream, and after we find out who loosed these robots on us, we can defeat them too. Then we can start again, building a society where the well-being of everyone is coupled with the prosperity of businesses."

Her father raised his eyebrows, studying her with an expression that looked slightly perplexed, but not affronted.

Since he refused to answer, she continued: "We can't return to the tyrants of the Milky Way, with their obsession with letting the government nose its way into every issue. Besides, what if the Ixa won the Second Galactic War? They certainly seemed likely to win it when we left. What if we return to find they've laid waste to the galaxy?"

"It is a chance we must take," Gi said. "Darkstream is too big for us to wrest control of the system from it in time. They will do as they did in the Milky Way: follow an ill-advised course until they have doomed us all. I understand that you fear government—I do, too. But you must understand that a fear of government will be inflated in one who has never known a government at all. The truth is that companies like Darkstream must be restrained in some way. Otherwise, they will subordinate everything to profit, including the health and security of the people."

Slowly, Lisa shook her head. "You are not the Gi Sato I know. The father I knew had a well-justified fear of government, and a respect for the importance of business."

"I still do—but I have always known that not every form of government is bad. I believe that if power is truly given to the people, good things can happen. It is through corruption that the true invasiveness occurs. I am not saying that business is bad, Lisa, or that it should be stamped out. Competition and commerce are vital parts of what it means to be human. You know that I have always emphasized the importance of self-interest."

"Yes..." Lisa said with reluctance.

"And I still do. But some thought must be devoted to finding a system that allows neither corporations nor governments to subvert the will of the people. A system that does not allow corporations to grow like a cancer, and one that forces the government to tend only to the needs of citizens."

Lisa shook her head. "I'm sorry, father. But I still must respectfully disagree." Without warning, the storm of emotion inside her became too much, and she walked away, leaving her father alone on the hilltop.

A transmission request came in as she made her way down the winding path, feeling worse and worse with each step. It was Marco Gonzalez.

"Lisa," he said when she put it through, overlaying reality with a faded version of his face. "I've broken the access controls for the mech sims. I can begin transferring them to you now, if you like."

"Yes, that will be fine. Thank you, Marco."

"Sure thing."

His face winked from existence, and Lisa cast a glance back at the hilltop, where her father still stood outside the shuttle, alone, staring after her.

For a moment, she almost went back to him. But she couldn't. Instead, she continued toward her army below.

CHAPTER 10

Electronic and Biological

The moment Ingress drew into view, its dew-covered steel walls glistening in the spreading dawn, Beth contacted Bronson.

She badly wanted to see Ash, and if they were going to make the space elevator before it began its daily trip up to Valhalla, they needed the go-ahead to do so in advance of their arrival.

Unfortunately, Bronson had other plans.

"You and Jin are to remain at Ingress," the captain's likeness said as it jogged alongside the MIMAS mechs. Inside the dream, Bronson's simulacrum was unbound by the rules of reality, and so it easily kept pace beside them.

"But, sir..." Beth said, and the officer glanced up at her sharply. She didn't make a habit of questioning orders, and no doubt it surprised Bronson to hear even the barest contradiction from her.

"Yes?" he asked tersely.

"We...we were hoping to return to Valhalla."

" *We* were hoping no such thing," Henrietta cut in. "This is all Arkanian."

Beth resisted the urge to glare at her fellow mech pilot.

"Interesting," Bronson muttered. "What value would there be in having you on the space station?"

"We could regroup with Steam," Beth said. "Plan Oneiri's next move."

"Oneiri is dead," Bronson answered. "You know that as well as I. We're already training your replacements. You and Jin here are nothing more than heavy assault units, now, and you're of far more use to me deployed planetside."

Beth cleared her throat, intent on trying one more time. "Sir—"

"I'm sorry, Seaman, I don't recall inviting you to debate the matter. It's like this: the force with which Gonzalez and Price have aligned themselves is currently advancing on Ingress, and I need every unit I can muster to defend the city. You'll be placed under the command of Captain Arkady Black, who's being given command of Darkstream's four remaining reserve battalions. I want you to find and report to him. *Now.* That's all."

With that, Bronson vanished from Eresos, returning his attention to wherever he happened to be. His destroyer, the *Javelin*, perhaps. Or maybe he was on Valhalla, with Ash.

"Do me a favor," Henrietta said, "and don't try to make me an accessory to reuniting with your crush."

The sky went ruby, and the color likely came pretty close to matching Beth's face, at the moment.

A notification sent to both their implants contained a code for gaining temporary access to Arkady Black's location, allowing them to follow Bronson's order promptly, as much as Beth had no desire to do so.

Orders were orders, though, and so they joined Black atop the city walls, where he was studying the lay of the land surrounding Ingress. They'd left their mechs on the ground below.

When they arrived, the captain turned slowly, taking them in with a steady gaze. "It's refreshing to speak with MIMAS pilots outside of their metal monstrosities," he said, somewhat wryly. "Although, I'm surprised to find you still possess the muscles necessary for walking under your own power."

"Yes, sir," Henrietta said, and Beth echoed the words, feeling resigned.

"Hmm. You both seem much more compliant than Roach did, not to mention Sweeney. Still, Bronson tells me that you came pretty close to betraying the company. Is that true?"

"No, sir," Henrietta said. "We were taking advantage of an opportunity to run recon on a new enemy force that was taking shape."

"Bronson told me you'd say that. That force certainly marshaled itself quickly, didn't it? Due in no small part, I'm sure, to the help of several former Darkstream employees. Tessa Notaras. Lisa Sato. Marco Gonzalez. Jake Price. You know two of those names quite well, don't you?"

"Yes, sir," Henrietta said, somewhat more haltingly than before.

"You worked closely with them. Shared meals with them. Fought alongside them, supported them, watched their backs. And now, just like that—" Black snapped his fingers "—they're your enemies. I can't decide which is worse: betraying your friends or betraying your employer. Which do you two consider worse?"

"Betraying your employer, *sir!*" Beth rattled off sharply, having noticed Henrietta wilting under Black's harsh tirade.

Beth's firmness seemed to rally Henrietta, and she repeated the words: "Betraying your employer is worse, sir!"

"That's exactly right, Jin. Arkanian. When your friends decided to go traitor, you made the right call to abandon them. I understand why you went to River Rock with them. You wanted to give them the benefit of the doubt—to hear them out. You fought with them, and you would have died with them, so you felt you owed them that much. But abandoning them when they lost their way...coming here to continue your service...that was the right call."

"Yes, sir," Henrietta said.

"That said, I'll be keeping a close eye on you, and I have eyes and ears all throughout this city, both electronic and biological. If you so much as dream about insubordination, I'll know it, and I'll have both of you court martialed so quickly your heads will spin. I hope I've made myself clear. Now, go report to Commander Cassandra Sora and see what work she has for you. I'll pass along additional orders for you shortly."

CHAPTER 11

Too Clever by Half

Jake carefully raised his head above the crest of the hill to take in the city that waited on the other side.

Twilight had nearly descended, and soon, the shadows would lengthen into night. Lisa's and Jake's hope was to take the city well before morning—before the space elevator was due to return to Valhalla Station.

It's going to be dicey.

Beside him, Marco also stole a glance at their target. Lower on the hill, two squads of Quatro waited, all of them armed, in case this reconnaissance mission was met with unexpected aggression.

But Ingress appeared to be closed-off, its defenders hunkered down inside to await the coming battle. Jake couldn't see anyone or anything outside of the city, which made sense. System net gossip said that Arkady Black had been given the command, and Jake expected only competence from a man like that.

If the resistance's goal had been to besiege Ingress, starving the city until it was forced to open its gates, Jake would have advocated for surrounding it and setting up camp while scouring the countryside for opportunities to keep their besieging army well-provisioned.

Unfortunately, they lacked the time for a siege, and even if there had been time, Ingress would have been basically impossible to starve out. With access to the space elevator, along with the rest of the solar system, it would have taken years to accomplish it, if not longer.

Plus, with growing armies of Amblers, Ravagers, and Gatherers marauding the countryside and engaging everything that moved, a siege was out of the question.

Instead, their objective would be to concentrate their firepower on one section of the city walls, with the aim of making it crumble and fall as quickly as possible. That done, they would take the city, secure the elevator, and ascend to Valhalla.

At least, that's the plan.

Andy Miller had insisted on tagging along for this scouting mission, and Jake hadn't been able to figure out why, considering the man had wanted nothing to do with Jake until now. Andy had talked one of the Quatro into letting him ride on his back—otherwise, he would never have been able to keep up on just his crutches.

As Jake descended the hillside to rejoin his Quatro escort, he soon discovered the reason for Andy's desire to accompany them. The man himself approached Jake directly, hobbling toward him as fast as he could, crutches swinging back and forth with abandon. He looked like he was spoiling for a confrontation of some kind.

Surely he's not stupid enough to try actually taking a swing at me. That would be embarrassing for both of them.

"Find something to do elsewhere, Spirit," Jake said to Marco. "This kid hates me, for whatever reason, but there's no need for you to get mixed up in it."

"Gotcha." Marco headed toward his MIMAS, which he'd left standing near the bottom of the hill.

"Andy," Jake said. "We'll be deploying soon. Shouldn't you get to the rear?"

Jake hadn't meant it as a slight, but Andy clearly took it as one. "I have just one thing to say to you," he said. "If you let anything happen to Lisa during the attack—*anything*—I'll do everything I can to kill you. I don't care how long I'll have to wait to do it, or what lengths I'll need to go to."

Jake cleared his throat, to mask the other reaction that threatened to exhibit itself. "I'm pretty sure Lisa can take care of herself," he said. "Isn't she the only reason you're still alive?"

"Just remember what I said," Andy spat, then turned to make his way carefully back down the hill.

I will remember it, Andy. But only as a pathetic attempt to intimidate me. One that does nothing to help our chances of winning the coming engagement.

Jake wasn't sure what Andy's problem was, but he did know that he pitied the man.

An unexpected transmission request came, then: from Captain Bob Bronson.

Jake only hesitated a moment before accepting.

Outside of the mech dream, Bronson appeared to him only as a head and shoulders superimposed over the real world by Jake's implant.

"Price. What are you doing?" The captain's voice dripped with scorn.

"It wouldn't make for very good OPSEC if I told you that, Bronson.

The man's mouth twisted, probably at Jake's failure to address him by rank. "I don't want to do this, but you've spooked the board. They want me to give you one last chance. Drop this hopeless crusade, boy, and take your job back. If you do that, everything will be forgotten. All you have to do is turn back your forces."

"You mistake why I joined the Darkstream military, Bronson. I know you think you recruited me with your promises of glory and riches, but that's not really why I joined. The real reasons were to help my sister get better and to pilot a mech. Sue Anne is dead now, and I'm still piloting a mech. I plan to use it to make you stop exploiting innocent people for profit. You don't have anything to offer me."

Bronson's eyes narrowed. "You're not just driving any mech. One of those things drove Roach mad, boy. You think you're helping people, but you don't know *what* you're doing. Your judgment's as compromised as Roach's was. Wake up, and get the hell out of that thing, before it's too late. Before you do something that strips away your humanity."

For a moment, Bronson's words actually gave Jake pause. *What if my judgment really has been compromised?* If it was, he probably wouldn't be aware of it, would he?

According to Marco, Roach had hallucinated that he was doing the right thing. It had led him to kill Richaud.

Am I just hallucinating that I'm fighting for a just cause?

But no. He could almost believe it, except that was exactly the sort of trick a man like Bronson would use to try to turn Jake against himself.

"You're too clever by half, Bronson. When I see you next, we won't be having a conversation." Jake cut off the transmission and started marching toward Lisa, who was approaching at the head of a battalion of Quatro.

He tried to calm himself down as much as he could—the conversation with Bronson had left him angry and bitter. Having to bring up his sister did that, and so did remembering how Bronson had ordered him to abandon his family to die in the attack on Hub. That was the reason Jake had gone against Darkstream in the first place.

"Jake," Lisa said. "Are you okay?"

"I'm fine. Let's get this moving, all right?"

"All right. What did you see up there?" She nodded toward the hilltop.

He was about to tell her about Bronson's offer, but he hesitated. He'd said no, and that would remain his answer, so to bring it up now could only plant a seed of doubt in Lisa's and the troops' minds. No matter how small a seed, it wasn't worth it.

"It's just like we expected. Ingress is locked up tight, and they haven't deployed any troops in the field. I think we should hit them from the southeast. The terrain is a bit hilly there, which will give us some cover from the snipers they've no doubt positioned along the walls. Plus, it happens to be our current approach vector. Redeploying to hit them from another direction will only give them more time to prepare."

"I agree," Lisa said, her expression grave. "I see no reason for any more delay. Let's begin."

CHAPTER 12

Signs of Insubordination

Ash woke to find Bronson looming over her bed, with two armed Darkstream marines standing at attention less than a meter behind him.

Why the escort? Does he think I'm a threat to him? "Captain," she said. Her voice was still quite hoarse, but it was getting stronger every day.

"Seaman," he said with a curt nod.

Her gaze drifted from Bronson's lined face to the pair of marines, and back again. "What's going on?"

"Ingress is under heavy assault. We're hoping the city garrison can repel them, especially given we've assigned the four remaining Darkstream reserve battalions to help out. But we're preparing for every possibility."

Ash blinked. "And that preparation involves me, somehow?"

"I'm afraid so. I know you're not fully recovered yet, but you don't need to be recovered to pilot a MIMAS. I'll have the best medical personnel on Valhalla administer measured doses of stims, to keep you alert. But I need you back in action."

Ash struggled to a sitting position, blinking away the grogginess that lingered. Most medical professionals still warned against using stims except in times of great need. "You're sending me down to Eresos, sir?"

"No, no. I wouldn't send you into *battle* in your condition, Sweeney. But I do want you to prepare some others for battle, in case the need arises."

"What others, sir?"

"The next group of MIMAS pilots have been selected. I want you to train them in on the mechs."

That made Ash fall silent for nearly a minute, as she considered Bronson's words. At last, she said, "You expect the attackers to take the elevator and make it up here, don't you, sir?"

"I expect nothing. But I intend to prepare for everything. That's my job—to get ready for any possibility. And to use everything I have at my disposal. I'm sorry to have to ask this of you, Sweeney. But I have to. I'm afraid it *is* an order."

"I understand, sir."

"There's something else. Before the Battle of Vanguard, you brought up a trove of documents that someone claimed was proof that Darkstream committed malfeasance. I told you the documents were fabricated. You've never shown any sign of insubordination before. You've always been a faithful soldier. But I worry that you let that crap impair your ability to think clearly. So I have to ask: do you accept that the documents were fabricated?"

"Yes, sir," Ash said quietly.

Bronson nodded, though he continued speaking: "We need a strong, unified Darkstream, Sweeney. Now more than ever. This insurrection is the last thing the people of the Steele System need."

The people of the Steele System are the last thing you'd give a damn about. This is about the company's bottom line, and nothing else.

But she didn't say any of that. "Yes, sir," she said instead.

CHAPTER 13

On Her Own Terms

T he steel walls muted the harsh staccato of gunfire, but colossal explosions boomed like thunder with unsettling regularity, shaking the guard tower more often than not.

Captain Arkady Black refused to stray far from the part of Ingress' walls where the enemy force was expected to strike.

Nothing compares with surveying the terrain with your own eyes. Satellite photos, maps, simulations—none of those came close.

His refusal to retreat to safer ground *was* unorthodox. Doctrine would have had him deep inside the city, preferably underground. Instead, he'd chosen the base of a guard tower that overlooked the field of battle.

He'd have chosen the top of the tower as his command post, but that would have caused his subordinates too much distress. This was his compromise.

Right now, he was using his implant to review a computer projection of how the coming engagement might unfold. The simulation was projected across an otherwise blank tabletop, and access to it was restricted only to him. Even another soldier with a Darkstream implant would see only a bare table.

The projection held no surprises—indeed, it conformed to his expectations. Its primary conclusion was identical to his: if he couldn't keep the enemy mechs away, the city walls would be breached before long. He had no way to reliably repel the mechs, so that was inevitable.

He also knew that far overhead, on Valhalla, Bronson was preparing for Black's defense to fail and for the barbarians at the gate to seize the space elevator. The final battle would be fought on the space station—both human judgment and computer projections agreed on the high probability of that.

I hope Bronson has something good ready for them.

An alert popped into existence over the simulated battlefield, telling him that Henrietta Jin was outside the tower, requesting permission to enter.

"Come in," he subvocalized.

The door slid upward into its casing, and Jin entered, looking small outside of her mech. She was above-average height, in reality, but he was used to interacting with the MIMAS pilots while they were inside their mechs. They seemed to live inside those things, or at least they did when they had free rein to do so. Black had found plenty of tasks for both Jin and Arkanian that required they leave their mechs, simply because he considered it good for them.

Jin came to attention and snapped off a salute that just missed the mark. If Black knew anything about officer-subordinate relations, the salute was calculated to be irksome but also just right enough that it didn't justify a reprimand.

Maybe that worked on other officers.

"Tighten up that salute, Jin. Did they let you MIMAS pilots skip Basic?"

"Sorry, sir."

"I want to see that salute again."

Jin snapped her hand to her temple, exhibiting much better form than before. Black gave a satisfied nod.

"Report," he said. "Is the operation I ordered complete?"

"Yes, Captain."

He paused, his gaze locked onto hers. "Are you ready to kill your friends?"

"Yes, sir."

"And the other one? Arkanian? Is *she* ready?"

"I believe so, Captain."

Black nodded again, then ran a hand across his cheek, which had sprouted some stubble. He didn't like that he'd grown lax with his personal grooming. It was sloppy, and it indicated to his soldiers that the coming engagement was affecting him.

"I've had my doubts about our mutual employer, too, you know," Black said after yet another pause. "Deep-seated doubts. I don't think Darkstream is a noble company. I don't even think they act responsibly, most of the time. But the difference between your friends and I is that *I* know what it is to follow orders. What is to be a loyal soldier. Even though I work for a corporation, that doesn't change what it means to be a soldier. Following orders is central to the *spirit* of that."

Black paused a moment to let his words sink in. It occurred to him that everything he'd said so far formed a well-worn argument for obeying one's superiors. And it wasn't even the extent of what he believed. So he dug deeper.

"The military is the last line of defense against chaos, Jin. That was true in the Milky Way, and it's especially true in the Steele System. Though the Darkstream military is not a tool that is used universally for good, if it falls apart, we're all doomed. Your friends haven't caught on to it yet, but they're the ones assaulting the security of all who live here—not us. Are you following me?"

Jin cleared her throat. "What if a soldier is given orders that should not be followed, sir?"

Black narrowed his eyes, studying Jin's neutral expression. "I need perfect compliance from you tonight, Jin. You've already chosen your path. Do you really plan to stray from it now?"

"No, sir."

The thunder of explosive ordnance rocked the tower once again.

"It's time for you to suit up," he said, taking a moment to relish how level his voice was.

"It's about damned time." Jin spun on her heel without waiting to be dismissed, slamming the access panel near the door with her palm, and marching out when it rose to let her pass.

She'll go to her death as ordered, but she'll do it on her own terms. Despite the speech he'd given, Black had to admit he admired that.

CHAPTER 14

It's Time

As Jake and pretty much everyone else had pointed out repeatedly, Lisa had marshaled this army, and she'd led it to victory once already. So it was only right that she retain command.

Maybe it feels right to them. All I want to do is vomit.

Mortar fire fell all around her, lighting up the dark and sending tremors through the ground. She tried to ignore the chaos and focus on the task at hand: commanding one of the largest armies Eresos had ever known.

An honor guard of Quatro surrounded her command post, behind the second-largest hill on the field of battle. She figured opting for the increased protection of the largest hill would have been too obvious, though she had ordered Quatro to come and go from behind it, as though receiving and carrying out orders. It even seemed to be working—enemy mortar fire was focused disproportionately on the larger rise.

Unfortunately, that didn't mean much in the grand scheme of things, since there was quite a lot of enemy mortar fire, in addition to a torrent of sniper fire and the occasional rocket. Black had clearly drilled into his men and women the importance of taking out Lisa's heavy artillery as quickly as possible, and Darkstream had obviously learned some valuable lessons from the previous Quatro attacks on Ingress and Plenitude.

Lisa had decided to forego tunneling into Ingress. Black would have already filled in the tunnel the quads had made, through which Rug's mate had gained entry to sew chaos in the city's streets. Lisa's own Quatro would have had to start digging anew, and she doubted there was enough time for that.

Luckily, her forces had access to quite a bit of artillery, most of it either taken from Darkstream patrols or raided from company outposts. As fierce a resistance as the city's defenders were putting up, they couldn't compensate for the numbers and might of the Quatro, or the fact that the walls were ultimately built to withstand only unarmed Quatro.

"Lisa," Tessa subvocalized over an encrypted channel. "We have visitors."

Lisa had put Tessa in charge of keeping an eye on their force's rear and flanks, as a precaution in case Darkstream had risked positioning a force out in the countryside to take them from behind.

"Are they hostile?" Lisa subvocalized.

"Negative. It's another Quatro drift—thirty or so, half of them armed, including three more rocket launchers."

"Excellent." During the march on Ingress, she'd sent Quatro runners in every direction, in a last-minute attempt to recruit even more soldiers for the coming battle. It seemed her efforts were paying off. Even thirty unarmed Quatro would have been the equivalent of dozens of human soldiers. Armed, they would prove invaluable.

"Get them up to speed as fast as you can and deploy them wherever you think they're needed most," Lisa said.

"Will do. Notaras out."

That taken care of, Lisa opened up another encrypted channel. "Jake. It's time."

"I'm on it," Jake said.

With that, three mechs—one MIMAS, one quad, and one bipedal monstrosity—charged from their various hiding spots, their suit lights dimmed so they didn't stand out too much in the night. The majority of Lisa's heavy-artillery-bearing Quatro were at their backs.

CHAPTER 15

Textbook

Jake charged forward, his forearms taking the shape of giant energy cannons, which he fired at the spot on the city walls that his HUD had painted in bright red. Those among the legion of Quatro with heavy artillery strapped to their backs fired on that spot too, and before long, the walls began to buckle and warp, though almost imperceptibly. If it hadn't been for his advanced night vision, Jake wasn't sure he would have been able to detect the effect they were having, especially in the darkness.

Fire from atop the city walls intensified, and the alien mech dream manifested a piercing violin note to notify him of two new arrivals to the battle: a pair of MIMAS mechs hurtling over the parapets to land with a ground-shaking *thud*.

Paste and Razor.

Jake ignored them, for now. They ran to engage the nearest mech—the quad piloted by Rug. As much as Jake wanted to assist, he knew breaching the walls had to be his top priority, and anyway, the Quatro could handle herself.

Twin rocket launchers took form from Jake's shoulders, loading and firing ordnance that he'd ordered the mech to fabricate in preparation for this battle. The effect of the resistance army's concentrated fire on the walls was palpable, now, and definitely visible to the naked eye. Even fortified steel wouldn't be able to take that kind of stress for much longer.

The enemy was focusing its fire principally on the mechs, which the dream translated as thousands of venomous hornet stings all across his torso and limbs.

Jake leapt forward several meters, barely dodging mortar fire. The explosion ruptured the ground behind him, along with the pair of unlucky Quatro that had been standing on it.

His rage made the sky flash scarlet, and the cursed whispers rose up in discordant harmony. He dashed toward Ingress, sprouting high, thin blades that glowed with intense heat. Plunging them both into the city walls, he strained to draw them apart.

Jake's anger crescendoed, and the bayonets disintegrated in a violent explosion of light and heat. Flames bathed Jake, but as the smoke cleared and his vision was restored, he saw that the walls had been breached, with a jagged gap large enough to admit three Quatro at a time.

He glanced behind him and saw several Quatro staggering across the battlefield, dazed, a couple of them injured.

I did that. He hadn't been aware the alien mech was capable of such a move, but he'd let himself be guided by his emotions, which was never a good idea when piloting the deadly machine.

Now, some of his allies had paid the price. He just hoped he hadn't done any permanent damage to them.

"Get back," he shouted at the injured Quatro, waving with enormous metal hands that had reformed in an instant. "You're in no condition to be at the front." Beyond those he addressed, the invading army was rushing forward to take the form of a wedge, which would funnel into Ingress as rapidly as possible.

A deafening *boom* sounded directly behind Jake, the shock-wave making him stagger forward several feet. He turned just in time to see another explosion, which was followed rapidly by dozens more, for hundreds of meters in opposite directions.

White-hot metal shrapnel screamed through the night, killing the Quatro he'd been concerned about, along with dozens more. Several pieces hit Jake, almost as painfully as the bullets had, and their size and force made him stumble backward.

An enormous stretch of wall was being blown outward onto the besieging army, visiting havoc upon their ranks. In several places, entire sections of the wall were blown free, crushing any who were unlucky enough to be nearby.

Jake shook his head, dazed. All across the battlefield, tiny fires blazed from the flaming shrapnel that had covered everything, and Quatro lay groaning and dying in every direction. Jake heard some human cries mixed in, too.

As his shock began to subside, he realized what Arkady Black had done. It wasn't hard to piece together, since it was unfolding before his very eyes.

Black had clearly known the city walls would be breached, and he'd accepted that—incorporated it into his tactics. So he'd blown it out himself, for nearly a kilometer, allowing his army to deploy onto the battlefield with lightning quickness. They were doing so now, and Jake soon saw the superior positioning Black's move had given them.

The defenders of Ingress were rushing forward to execute a flanking maneuver more perfect than any Jake remembered from the military history texts he'd devoured while on Valhalla. Tanks were concentrated at the edges of Black's force, and they began to hammer the Quatro with explosive anti-tank rounds.

CHAPTER 16

This Is Awkward

For Jake, the only response that made sense to such an unexpected move was a decisive counterattack.

"To me!" he boomed, using the mech to amplify his voice a hundredfold. "Everyone, to me!" With that, Jake barreled toward the rightmost pincer of Black's flank, his arms morphing into heavy machine guns he planned to use to rip up the human ranks.

To their credit, the Quatro rallied quickly, forming themselves into a great, purple javelin to strike at the heart of what amounted to half of the enemy forces.

With any luck, they'd rapidly disable that formation, and the enemy flanking maneuver would fall apart. Jake began directing his remaining rockets at the tanks, though it took five just to neutralize one of them.

Black was smart, and he'd spread his tanks out, meaning the resistance mechs couldn't deal with them easily.

Worse, Black had also dispersed his mortar teams directly behind his forces, and they rained holy hell onto the Quatro ar-

my, landing mortar bombs in random locations and taking out
multiple targets more often than not.

Most devastating was the fact that the leftmost pincer was
recovering quickly from Jake's swift reaction, spreading out behind his and Lisa's forces to envelop them.

That's not good. If the Ingress defenders maintained a superior firing arc for too long, Jake knew the day would be lost, and
the resistance would end in fire and death. He doubted
Darkstream intended to take many prisoners from among the
alien army.

The state of play on the battlefield shifted rapidly, and without warning, Jake came face to face with the MIMAS mechs piloted by Beth and Henrietta. They both gripped their heavy
machine guns, and the moment they saw him they whipped the
muzzles toward his head, though they didn't fire. Not yet.

Jake did not raise his weapons in kind. "Razor. Paste. I don't
want to hurt you."

"It's sort of part of the job at this point, Jake," Henrietta said,
and inside his mech, he winced at her failure to use his Oneiri
nickname.

"Seems a bit senseless, after having each other's back for so
long," he answered, trying to decide whether he sounded like he
was begging or not. "I don't *want* to fight you," he said, and he
heard his own voice hitch. "I've already watched the people I
love suffer way too much. I really don't want to become just another source of that suffering."

The head of Henrietta's mech twitched toward Beth's. "Maybe he's right."

Beth replaced her heavy machine gun on her back. Then, with a strangled yell, she extended both her bayonets and charged straight at him.

Lightning-quick, his machine gun forearms became rounded shields instead. He raised his right shield to parry Beth's first blow, but her second carried such force that it punctured his left shield, the blade's point coming to within centimeters of his face. Even inside the mech dream, Jake felt his eyes go cross-eyed for the fraction of a second that he stared at it.

He wrenched the skewered shield to the left, jerking Beth's arm along with it. The blade slid out, bending slightly but not snapping, and Beth staggered.

An anti-tank round connected squarely with Jake's right side, throwing him backward against a Quatro who was firing on a squad of soldiers clustered near the city walls. The great alien shrieked in pain as the larger alien mech slammed it to the ground, and Jake felt something inside the Quatro's body give way with a *crunch.*

"Sorry!" he yelled, cringing at the damage he'd done, but even if he'd known how, there wasn't time to minister to the Quatro, or even to make sure it was okay. The side of his mech yawned open from the anti-tank round, and though it was in the process of quickly knitting itself back together, Beth had renewed her vicious assault.

For her part, Henrietta was circling around, her heavy machine gun still raised and pointing at him. "Sorry, Jake," she said, squeezing the trigger. His head jerked back with the impact of her burst, and the mech dream represented it as an instant headache, worse than any migraine he'd ever experienced.

But he couldn't let it slow him down. Beth was bringing both bayonets to bear once again, forcing Jake back on his heels as he swayed left and right to dodge her thrusts, like a champion boxer about to lose his title.

Henrietta continued to send heavy ordnance into his right side, and now she started focusing on the spot where the tank round had hit him, her bullets drilling closer and closer to where Jake's body rested inside the alien mech.

His vision blurred, and the dream simulated his own heartbeat pounding in his ears. Bringing his arms apart in a sweeping gesture, Jake knocked both of Beth's bayonets aside. He shoved her, sending her reeling backward. "How *could* you?" he screamed. "We're teammates, damn you both! Are Darkstream's profits more important to you?"

"That thing you pilot will drive you insane, Jake," Beth yelled back. "Roach's mech turned him into a mad dog, and he ran Ash through. He nearly killed her. You were lost to us the moment you climbed inside that mech."

Beth charged forward once again, her left blade aimed at Jake's head. He barely knocked it aside, dancing backward to avoid a slice from the other bayonet.

But he still couldn't bring himself to fight. He kept thinking of Sue Anne's face, racked with pain from her illness. He thought of his mother, and his father, and everything his neighbors back in Hub had gone through.

I can't be the cause of more pain for the people I love. He couldn't, though he cursed himself for a fool that he continued to love the people trying to kill him.

The battle raged around them, and Black's forces enveloped Lisa's. Henrietta sidestepped smoothly to get a better angle around Beth. She opened up on Jake, sending round after round into his wounded side, preventing it from repairing properly. Her bullets tunneled closer and closer to him.

They're going to kill me. Black ordered them to, and they're really going to do it.

Rug drew into view behind Henrietta, and for Jake, everything seemed to slow, as though encased in thick gel. An energy cannon sprouted from Rug's chest, aimed at Henrietta. The Quatro seemed to share none of Jake's hangups when it came to returning the MIMAS pilots' hostility.

"Rug, *no!*" Jake shouted.

Too late. A massive blast of energy sprouted from her gun, taking Henrietta's left arm clean off, and causing her heavy gun to tumble to the ground.

Despite the pain Jake knew the mech dream must have been communicating after losing the MIMAS' arm, Henrietta wasted no time in reacting. She swung her right arm around, its fingers retracting against her wrist to expose the rotary autocannon beneath, and she pelted Rug with it, causing the alien to flinch backward.

Something was changing on the battlefield. The volume behind Jake had dropped, and the amount of ordnance coming from that direction had lessened, too.

He turned to take in the reason why. Lisa's efforts to recruit more Quatro drifts to their cause had paid off in dividends, and just in time, it seemed.

A second force had arrived—just under half of the existing Quatro force, by Jake's estimation—and they were pounding Black's left pincer, eviscerating what had been a devastating flanking maneuver mere moments ago.

Jake's rear sensors alerted him to a renewed assault from Beth, and he turned to answer it, but then she suddenly dropped both arms.

He kept his arms up, wary that this was a ploy of some kind. Except, he noticed more Darkstream soldiers beyond Beth dropping their weapons as well, and raising their hands toward the sky.

"Black just ordered the surrender," she said, her tone flat. "He can recognize a rout when he sees one."

"I see," Jake said, finally lowering his arms too. He glanced from Beth to Henrietta, and then back at Beth again. "Well, this is awkward."

CHAPTER 17

Repelling the Actual Attack

Their training clearly wasn't like what Roach put us through, Ash reflected as she watched the MIMAS trainees coordinate a mock assault against a simulated enemy's position on Valhalla's Endless Beach.

The new MIMAS team had chosen the name Phantom, which Ash didn't think fit very well. Either way, their coordination was lackluster, coming nowhere close to the hairpin tactical pivots Oneiri Team had executed on a regular basis. It was Ash's job to teach them to emulate that level of responsiveness, she supposed, but the material she had to work with was a far cry from the hardened weapons that Roach's training had made of Ash and the others.

Of course, she still wasn't prepared to think of what Roach had done to them as humane, but maybe it had come close to being justified. She wouldn't have said that at the time, but now she felt grateful that she'd become tough enough to endure the horrors that Eresos had subjected Oneiri to.

Few of her memories involving Roach were fond ones. But for this, she did offer him quiet thanks.

"Tighten up that formation," she barked into the coms of the five mechs making up the sneak attack's main thrust.

"Sneak attack" had been their term, not hers, and it wasn't exactly what she would have called it. Any enemy commander worth his or her salt would have handily anticipated an attack from the trajectory they'd chosen, which made it wholly unsurprising when the simulated enemy succeeded in surrounding the MIMAS pilots. That done, they began tearing them apart.

Ash fought her mounting agitation, which urged her to chew them out for the eighth time this week. Instead, she started pacing her own mech up and down the sand.

Maybe it's a good thing their training wasn't as rigorous as ours. She remembered rumors that the Darkstream brass hadn't liked how rough Roach had been on them, and they'd likely scrapped his program for one of their own design.

Did she actually want to try to fix the bad habits the new pilots had been left with? *Do I really want to improve the soldiers who'll be ordered to kill my friends?*

A few of the new pilots *were* capable soldiers, despite Darkstream's bungling. Ash had seen early on how well-rounded Seaman Apprentice Maura Odell was. Her only real shortcoming was being lumped in with a team that lacked cohesion. Orson Cole had a keen tactical mind, but he wasn't persuasive enough to sell his ideas to his teammates, who couldn't appreciate their value. And Benny Cho was a dead shot who really should have been providing fire support in the current exercise, rather than leading the frontal assault.

The simulated enemy routed Phantom Team, and Ash suppressed a sigh as they approached her slowly, no doubt reluctant to hear her views about what had just gone on.

The weaker they are, the less of a danger they'll be to Jake and Marco, Ash reminded herself. Still, it was hard to watch soldiers falling apart when she was responsible for forging them into an effective weapon.

"I know I don't need to break down the mess you just made of that," she said when the eight mechs were assembled before her. "You repeated every mistake I've pointed out to you from previous exercises. It's like you went out of your way not to miss a single mistake." She shook her head. "Everyone to your bunks. We're going lucid. Your situational awareness needs a *lot* of work." Lucid was ideally suited to that, since it lent authenticity to the emotional component of simulations.

But that wasn't her only reason for choosing to conduct this exercise using lucid—nor was it her main reason. Though Darkstream logged everything that happened in lucid, Ash knew they were much laxer when it came to reviewing it than they were with actual events recorded by soldiers' implants. That made it even less likely that they'd catch on to what she was really trying to accomplish.

"Officially, I'm not supposed to discuss this with you," Ash said once the team was once again assembled before her, this time inside the dream. "But it's no real secret that a resistance force is attacking Ingress, led by MIMAS pilots who have gone rogue. So I might as well use it to guide your training. There's a chance that the traitors will secure the elevator and use it to attack Valhalla. What I want you to do is design the type of defense that you'd recommend for the station's garrison to use, and then implement it against a simulated attack. There are no wrong answers, here. If you consider surrender or retreat to be the most viable route, then say so, but justify your response. And know that you're going to look pretty stupid if you advocate retreat while your teammate organizes a defense that holds out against my simulated attack." Ash smiled. "Now get to work."

She'd intentionally phrased the exercise in a way that sounded like she was discouraging retreat, and it was possible none of them would choose that route. Even so, judging by how conservative each pilot's defense turned out to be, she'd be able to gauge just how optimistic they were about Valhalla's chances of repelling the actual attack.

Her true aim was to figure out which pilots were most pessimistic about Darkstream's victory. Those would also be the ones most likely to join Jake's side when the time came.

CHAPTER 18

Imminent Doom

This should be pleasant, Jake thought sardonically.

Lisa had directed Black to meet her and her officers in a large plaza near the wall he'd obliterated. Who her officers actually were was a little hazy, and something Lisa was, of necessity, figuring out on the fly. All Jake knew was that he was one of them.

"Order the enemy MIMAS pilots to get out of their mechs," Lisa had instructed him over a private channel. "I'm assigning twenty Quatro to guard the mechs themselves. I want you to take both pilots with you to the meeting. Keep them close."

"Will do," he'd said.

He was certain Lisa had chosen the plaza as their meeting place for symbolic reasons, since otherwise it didn't actually matter where Black delivered his formal surrender. Having him do so inside the actual city underscored Darkstream's defeat, and would hopefully circumvent any thoughts among the company forces of going against Black's decision.

Jake, Marco, and Rug remained inside their respective mechs, and they escorted Beth and Henrietta toward Ingress in silence, other than the brittle grass that crackled underfoot.

Jake considered telling Beth that Ash was on his side—that she'd tipped him off about Bronson's maniacal talk of nuking the planet to defeat the robots. But he decided there was no point. The damage had already been done, to his relationship with both Beth and Henrietta.

Besides, if anyone with Darkstream finds out that Ash helped me, it could endanger her. Bronson is just one covert transmission away.

As they neared the wall—or rather, where the wall once had stood—the going became much slower, mainly because of the obstacle the rubble posed to Beth and Henrietta. Without their mechs, they were forced to pick their way over twisted shards of steel that would have posed little risk to a MIMAS. They took it in stride, though, uncomplaining. If he was being honest with himself, Jake had to admit that he hadn't expected anything less from them. As betrayed as he felt, his estimation of the two women's proficiency had not fallen.

At last they drew clear of the rubble, and soon after that the plaza came into view, with its growing gathering of officers. Lisa was already there, along with Tessa Notaras and the leaders of several Quatro drifts. Black was also waiting, with several of his officers, most of whom Jake recognized. Commander Cassandra Odell was present, too, who commanded the Ingress garrison.

As Jake neared them, he saw the shell-shocked expressions worn by Lisa and several of the others, including many among the Darkstream military personnel.

"What's going on?" Jake asked when he reached them.

Lisa cleared her throat. "Captain Black has just informed me that he surrendered partly because of an enormous host of robots that has been spotted advancing on the city."

Overhead, the sky went blood-red, even though dawn was still several hours off. Jake could feel sweat trickling down his back, or at least the mech simulated the sensation. *It's better than the coat of insects it treated me to back in Hub.*

He turned to Arkady Black. "How long till the robots get here?"

Black sniffed, his manner closer to someone discussing the advent of some unfavorable weather rather than someone discussing the imminent doom of himself and those around him. "Less than two hours, by our best estimate."

CHAPTER 19

A Pair of Rockets

"So we have two hours to coordinate the defense of Eresos' largest city, against a legion of killer robots," Jake said.

"That's correct," Black answered.

"Then maybe blowing the walls apart wasn't the best idea!" Jake shot back, unable to keep his voice from rising sharply in volume.

Black shrugged. "I had no idea your treacherous attack would be followed be a second wave of metal attackers. Blowing the walls was the only path I saw to victory against you—it was our only viable option. Doing so enabled me to effectively employ force concentration against you, and it would have worked had it not been for the incredibly lucky arrival of your reinforcements."

Jake fell silent, then, fighting the urge to shift his weight under the gaze of everyone present. In truth, he wasn't sure he could have done much better than Black, if he'd been charged with the defense of Ingress. And Black was right—the extra Quatro's arrival *had* been extremely fortunate.

Black is a talented battle commander. Probably Darkstream's best.

Lisa seemed to recognize that, too. "Captain Black, are you willing to work together with us to repel the coming robot assault?"

Black nodded. "I am."

Henrietta looked at Lisa with what wasn't quite a glare. "Can I have leave to return to my mech?"

After a moment's consideration, Lisa nodded. "You have my leave. Until this battle is over, I see no reason not to give your weapon back to you. Circumstances have afforded us a bond of trust, however temporary."

"That's right," Henrietta said. "We won't stab you in the back like you did to Darkstream." With that, she stormed off, and Beth followed, studiously avoiding eye contact with Jake.

"Relay the situation to the reserve battalion commanders," Black called after the MIMAS pilots. "Deploy wherever they tell you to." He turned to Lisa. "My destruction of the walls *does* present a number of unique challenges, now. The enemy will no doubt concentrate their forces there, but they could easily blow holes in other parts of the wall as well. We'll have to cluster most of our units near the breach, of course, but we will also need an even distribution of defenders atop the undamaged sections."

Lisa nodded. "You're right. Let's keep all the tanks next to the breach, but position your mortar teams along the walls, in such a way that allows them to rapidly respond to pressure inflicted by the enemy."

"Exactly what I was going to suggest," Black said, and Jake thought he even sounded a bit impressed.

"Captain Black, I leave it to you to coordinate the defense of the unbroken walls," Lisa said. "I will take command of the forces at the breach."

Black nodded. "Seems as good an arrangement as any."

Jake didn't think his tone inspired much hope in anyone.

At first, the members of Lisa's command structure were silent on the way back to the battlefield. But halfway there, Tessa Notaras spoke up, mostly directing her speech at Lisa:

"I've been skimming the system net," she said, her jaw tight. "There are reports of settlements all over the planet being overrun by the bots. It always seems to start with Gatherers turning violent as they enter or exit the resource collection sites. They take out as many people as they can before they're taken out themselves. Shortly after that, with the village still weakened and reeling, the Amblers and Ravagers hit."

Lisa shook her head, her expression akin to nausea.

One of the Quatro leaders spoke up—Salve, whose drift Jake knew Lisa had recruited from the lands to the east of the Barrens. "We aimed to take Ingress in order to give the people of this planet some security from Darkstream. Instead, it seems we must use the elevator ourselves, as our last and only avenue of escape from the robots."

"We're not abandoning Eresos," Lisa said, her voice firming up. "We'll repel this wave of attackers, then we'll deploy to the countryside and save the people who live there."

Tessa was shaking her head. "I don't think there's going to be much left to save, Lisa. The reports are flooding in of villages being wiped off the map. Almost every attack has inflicted one hundred percent casualty rates."

Lisa had no answer for that.

Rug spoke up, her eyes glowing softly in the pre-dawn darkness: "Tessa Notaras is right, Lisa Sato. We are spending our lives needlessly in fighting this battle for Darkstream. We must escape while we still can."

"It's never a waste when you're fighting to protect people," Lisa said. "We're staying."

"I agree," Jake said, and though it was all he could think to say, Lisa seemed to appreciate his words.

She smiled up at him. "Thank you, Jake."

He nodded. "We made you commander, and we don't get to change that just because we might not like your orders. Personally, I *do* like them. Let's save this city."

They reached the curved line of rubble that used to be Ingress' walls, where resistance and Darkstream soldiers had already widened paths to facilitate a more orderly retreat into the city, in case that became necessary.

It didn't take long for Jake to spot Beth and Henrietta, towering above the other soldiers and even the other vehicles in their MIMAS mechs. They were both digging trenches at the front of the battlefield, using their bayonets to loosen the earth and then employing cupped metal hands to scoop it to the front, in a fashion that looked surprisingly efficient, even despite Henrietta's missing arm.

Jake noticed many of the soldiers glancing at the mechs frequently, and their spirits seemed to lift whenever they did.

The mechs are giving them hope, he realized. Since being deployed to Eresos, he hadn't spent a lot of time among regular infantry, and when he had, he'd only had reason to believe that they resented the MIMAS pilots. But now, in what was probably their most desperate hour, the mechs' show of vigor and might seemed to be one of the only things keeping the fighting men and women going.

Seeing former Oneiri members live up to what Oneiri was originally meant to be about...it didn't seem to fit with his anger over Beth's and Henrietta's willingness to try to kill him.

Could Oneiri ever get back together? He wanted to punch himself for even having that thought, or for daring to hope for it. But if it served the people of the Steele System...shouldn't he try to get past what they'd done to him?

"Contact!" someone yelled, riveting Jake's eyes to the horizon. An Ambler was striding rapidly into view, its broad dome of a head bobbing as it crested the horizon.

Another dome appeared a few dozen meters to the left, and another rose over the steep hill where the quads had attempted to tunnel into Ingress during a previous attack on the city.

They're here. Ahead of schedule.

Next, the horizon seemed to writhe, as though it had come alive. Jake instructed the mech's sensors to zoom in, and he saw that the ground was covered with Gatherers. A minute later, swarms of Ravagers followed, striding among their squat fellows.

The entire metallic mass seethed forward.

"Open fire!" Lisa shouted over the coms. Jake wasn't sure whether she'd been given access to Darkstream channels, but it didn't matter. Once the shooting began, everyone got the message, pumping round after round into the oncoming legion.

Well before this battle, Jake and others had noted a self-preservation instinct in the planet's robotic former servants. That instinct did not appear to be in effect today. The concentrated fire of the resistance and Darkstream quickly took out one Ambler, then another, not to mention countless smaller robots. But it didn't seem to matter. More Amblers rose over the horizon to replace the ones that had fallen, and the Ravagers charged forward.

The word "charged" didn't seem to fit the movement of the Gatherers, though—it was more like crawling. Their lowness served them well, as did the fact that individually, they were fairly low-value targets. As a result, the human soldiers all focused on the taller robots, leaving the Gatherers to sweep forward, quickly closing the distance.

Jake attempted to rectify that, peppering the front ranks of Gatherers with energy blasts, which he tried to calibrate as conservatively as possible while still taking out multiple Gatherers at a time. Rug caught on to the tactic, mimicking it, and Marco followed suit with both of his rotary autocannons.

It made no difference. The front of the robot host surged forward, and before long, they were crawling into the trenches with the soldiers. Most of the men and women who'd been crouched there scrambled out, backing toward the city while firing into the metal masses. The braver ones—or perhaps the more foolhardy ones—stayed to fight it out, and Jake's enhanced vision allowed him to see the blood that spurted into the air all along the makeshift fortification.

The advent of the Gatherers drew the attention of most of the soldiers, which lessened the pressure on the Ravagers and Amblers, who also started getting closer.

Abruptly, contrary to their name, the Amblers charged forward, metal feet pounding across the earth. Within seconds they were among the front ranks of infantry, getting hammered by anti-tank round after anti-tank round. Several more of the autonomous mechs went down, but there were too many of them, and the combined Darkstream and resistance fighters were thrown into chaos by the robots in their midst.

"Retreat!" came Lisa's voice over the com. "Back into the city!"

The front ranks were doomed, and most of the soldiers that comprised them seemed to recognize it. In an incredible show of bravery, most of them fought on with increased vigor, spending their final moments to buy time for the rest of the force to fall back into the city while firing on the robots.

Jake dashed forward to help with the effort to stem the metal tide, and so did Henrietta, Beth, Marco, and Rug. Alien, quad, and MIMAS mech alike hit the enemy with everything, and the adrenaline surging through Jake's veins was unlike anything he'd experienced in a long time. Thrills shot through him as they worked together to take down Ambler after Ambler using heavy gunfire, rockets, lasers, and energy blasts.

Except for Henrietta—instead, she laid about the enemy with her single remaining blade, demonstrating once more why her teammates had christened her "Razor."

Ravager after Ravager exploded into showers of metal fragments as she cut through them in midair. Henrietta had also retracted her hand to reveal the autocannon beneath, and she managed to incorporate it into her swordplay to maximize the damage she was dealing to the enemy.

Jake tried not to let her dazzling display distract him from his own efforts to hold back the enemy, but he couldn't help marveling as Henrietta rocketed into the air, coming down on top of an Ambler and driving her bayonet into its dome while sending high-velocity rounds burrowing deep inside its brain. The Ambler crumpled to the ground, and she turned to confront the next.

It hit her with a pair of rockets at point-blank range, sending her hurtling backward onto the ground.

As she struggled to rise to her feet, the Ambler stepped forward, firing two more rockets, heedless of the damage it was itself taking by deploying the explosives at such proximity.

Battered and smoking, Henrietta manage to raise her rotary autocannon to fire on her adversary. But even as she fired, Ravagers took advantage of her supine position, crawling all over her mech to rip it apart.

Jake knew from experience how quickly you needed to deal with Ravagers to prevent them from compromising your mech. He also knew, as he barreled across the battlefield to help his former teammate, that he was far too late.

A Ravager disappeared inside the MIMAS' torso, followed by a spray of blood. Henrietta's blood.

Jake yelled, his blood pounding in his ears, both arms becoming energy cannons to melt the Ambler who'd downed Razor and to disintegrate the Ravagers who'd killed her.

But nothing could bring her back—and, he realized, nothing could bring Oneiri back.

CHAPTER 20

Commit More Horrors

Well, that's interesting, Ash thought as she reviewed an encrypted message from a friend she'd sometimes gotten coffee with during the scant free time Roach's training had afforded her.

As creepy and invasive as Darkstream was, the technology they used to spy on people went both ways. The very employees they tasked with learning the secrets of others also had the ability and resources to access the company's own secrets, and it only took one person to leak those secrets, so that everyone knew them.

That was why, despite Darkstream's best efforts, rumors spread so quickly across Valhalla. And across the Steele System as a whole.

Not that there's much left of the system for them to spread across, Ash reflected, her lips pursed.

The rumor her old coffee buddy had shared with her had to do with the remains of Gabriel Roach, which Darkstream had plucked off the killing field outside Vanguard and transported back up to the station for study.

Or at least, they were supposed to be Roach's remains. According to the rumor, Roach was exhibiting signs of not actually being dead. Energy signatures, brain waves, screamed threats of torture and death—the rumor wasn't clear on what those signs actually were, but it did seem pretty confident that Darkstream had discovered a way to keep Roach contained.

That made sense, of course. If he was alive and they *hadn't* been able to contain him, Ash felt pretty confident the rumor would have quickly become solid fact, in the form of Roach rampaging through the station, killing everything in sight.

She decided to try investigating the matter herself. That night, she took an REM sleep-inducing sedative and soon found herself in the lucid lobby she'd configured a long time ago. That done, she began running through a series of transmission codes she had for Roach, starting with the most public and ending with a code that had been distributed only to members of Oneiri.

The final code worked. She established a connection over lucid, and within minutes she found herself on a barren, gray planetoid—inside of her MIMAS. Even in lucid, her instinct was to come as prepared as possible to deal with her old commander.

The decision turned out to be a lucky one, since this place had no breathable atmosphere. The dream would have rendered the experience of suffocating with the same authenticity it did everything else, and while it couldn't actually hurt her, it would have been extremely unpleasant.

Ahead of her walked the alien mech that was now Roach, his back turned to her. She sensed that he was aware of her presence, though.

"Where is this place?" she called.

"It's Earth's moon," he answered, and the mech dream conveyed his words to her. Otherwise, the lack of atmosphere would have rendered communication impossible. "Being here makes me feel exactly as alone as I want to be."

"Good for you," she said.

"Why have you come here?"

Ash shook her head. "What incentive do I have to tell you anything?"

That made Roach stop walking and turn to face her. "Good point." His face was as impassive as only an alien mech's could be. That was one of the challenges of interacting while inside mechs—other than body language, everyone was essentially unreadable.

"I owe you an apology," he said.

"You owe me a lot more than that."

"I know. You have no reason to trust me, and certainly no reason to respect me. I betrayed you in the deepest, most unforgivable way. And so I have to ask again: why are you here?"

"Curiosity, mostly. I heard you might still be alive."

Roach nodded. "Turns out I am. Unfortunately."

"Hatching another plan to avenge my sister, maybe? Going to refashion yourself as the wronged man, crusading for justice and vengeance? You seemed to enjoy playing that role before."

The alien mech shook its head. "No. I'm not even worthy to speak your sister's name, let alone pretend that I'm suited to bring about some kind of justice. I was messed up long before Jess died, Ash. I've committed a lot of crimes in Darkstream's employ—perpetrated a lot of atrocities. I didn't know it had affected me so much, but I've had a lot of time to think. I've started to realize that I was using vengeance as a vehicle for the rage I've built up over the course of decades. Rage at myself, mostly."

Ash nodded. "How nice for you, that you've had this epiphany. No doubt it's positioned you to convincingly atone for everything you've done. I'm sure everyone will jump right on board as you humbly work to redeem yourself. I just can't wait to watch you come back to us, Roach." Ash wasn't used to being this bitter, and she was surprised by how easily it came to her.

Roach shook his head. "You don't understand. I have no illusions about redemption. Actually, I wish Jake truly had killed me back at Vanguard. I don't trust myself to be alive. I'm frightened I'll commit more horrors—actually, I'm sure of it. Except, Darkstream seems to have found a way to restrain me. I haven't figured out how to break the bonds they've put on me, and I don't want to figure it out."

"Well, too bad," Ash spat. "Freeing you suits my purposes, so I *do* plan to find a way."

For a moment, Roach froze in spot. Then, he raised his hands toward her. "No, Ash. Please. I don't want my freedom back. This thing has corrupted me. I can't control myself anymore."

"That's exactly what I'm counting on." With that, Ash departed lucid.

CHAPTER 21

The Brightening Sky

Lisa swapped out her SL-17's empty magazine for a full one and continued firing on the endless metal legion pouring over the staggered mound of rubble that once had been the city's walls.

The combined resistance and Darkstream armies were fighting in the streets of Ingress now, using the buildings themselves for cover. Of course, that only worked for so long—the Amblers had no qualms about blasting homes and businesses to pieces.

It quickly became clear that no effort had been made to evacuate the civilian population in advance of the resistance's attack, and now, it was far too late. Citizens fled from the buildings the robots hit, stumbling from shock, faces white with terror. Lisa didn't like to think about the ones who hadn't had the chance to make it out at all.

An Ambler's guns blazed, hitting the building directly behind her, two meters overhead. She glanced back to spot a piece of its wall tumbling down at her, and she sprinted forward—

away from the immediate danger but toward the metal attack-ers.

With no one to cover her but herself, she unloaded into a pair of nearby Ravagers, who'd seemed to lock onto her right away, charging toward her. Two full rounds saw to the first one, but the steel claws of the second came within inches of her face be-fore she managed to fell it.

Dawn was starting to break across the city, which at least made the robotic attackers a little easier to pick out. Lisa wasn't convinced it was a positive, overall, though—it only gave a clearer picture of the city's doom, which wouldn't do much for morale.

Morale is barely a factor, anymore. We're done here.

Every so often, Lisa had been checking over her shoulder to ensure the space elevator wasn't leaving. Its schedule involved workers loading it up with cargo overnight for a morning de-parture, and while Lisa felt certain the night's events would dis-rupt that schedule, she wasn't confident it would disrupt it in the resistance's favor.

Indeed, when she looked over her shoulder again, she saw that the elevator had begun its climb toward Valhalla.

Damn it. I need to deal with that.

She focused on safely extracting herself from the fighting while she sent a transmission request to Arkady Black. To her surprise, he answered.

"Black. Did you order that elevator to ascend without us?"

"I did not," he said. "But you can hardly expect Darkstream to order its operators to keep it on the ground so that you can stroll onto it."

Black's sarcasm-laced calm was starting to get to her, but she had to admit she was impressed by his ability to maintain it in the face of overwhelming odds. She shook her head a little, to clear it. "We're leaving," she said. "Will you try to impede us?"

"No," Black said. "But I would remind you that if you do succeed in leaving, you'll be abandoning my soldiers and I to our deaths, along with the people of Ingress."

"Don't try to put that on me," Lisa snapped. "They should have been evacuated the moment you were notified of our attack."

"Well, they were not, and it wasn't my call to make. Leaving us here, on the other hand, is *wholly* your responsibility. And I don't think it will allow you to rest easy, for many years to come."

Lisa gripped her assault rifle harder. Black was right, but it didn't change their situation. Ingress was lost, and it was looking increasingly likely that the entire planet was also lost.

"Good luck, Black," she said at last. "Thank you for your assistance until now."

"And thank you for your empty words." Black terminated the transmission.

Drawing a deep breath, Lisa reached out to Jake over a one-to-one encrypted channel. "Jake. Did you notice our ride leaving?"

"I did," he said over the sound of his energy cannons firing.

"I need you to rocket up there and bring it back to us. In the meantime, I'm hauling our troops back to the elevator's base and holding that area for as long as I need to."

"Understood," Jake said.

Seconds later, Lisa spotted him against the brightening sky, gouts of flame streaming from his arms and legs.

CHAPTER 22

Surrender, Then

The space elevator had already been dwindling to a speck when Jake began rocketing toward it. That changed as the alien mech's rockets hurled him into the sky, and the great disk of the elevator's underside blossomed in his sights.

The adrenaline surging through his body made him want to blast the elevator to pieces with massive bolts of energy, and the whispers had already risen in unison to encourage that sentiment.

I think it could prove contrary to our objectives, Jake thought wryly, and his mirth silenced the whispers. Humor often proved an effective antidote to them—as though they were offended by the fact that their efforts to corrupt amused him.

But they did. The idea that he would go against his dead sister's wishes by embracing their invitation to merge into a single being with the mech...it really was laughable. The whispers claimed his powers would be augmented by doing so, and Jake believed that. He did find the promise of more power seductive, because that would make him more effective against

Darkstream, as well as the robots that were wreaking such destruction on humanity.

But he knew that if he accepted the offer, in time *he* would prove the most destructive to those he loved. That was something he simply couldn't allow.

Your confidence is what will cause you to succumb, one of the whispers hissed threateningly. None of the whispers had adopted quite that tone with him before, and it was unusual for just one of them to speak alone like that.

It took him aback, which was unfortunate, given the timing—just as he reached the elevator doors, which were sealed shut against him.

He shook himself to clear his head, and as he did, he flashed back to his escape from the Javelin, when his hands had become wedges to wrench the airlock doors apart. Now, he did the same, sliding the ultra-thin tips between the sealed doors.

Pulling his arms apart, he felt something inside the door break. *Damn it.* His aim hadn't been to disable the locking mechanism, but he feared that was exactly what he'd done.

Nothing for it. If the resistance army couldn't use the space elevator to ascend, they would be overrun, so Jake had to behave as though it was still a possibility. It wasn't constructive to do anything else.

Inside the elevator, he found two squads' worth of Darkstream soldiers from one of the reserve battalions that had been deployed to defend Ingress.

That cast a red filter over everything Jake could see. The fact that these cowards had left the city while the civilians they'd failed to evacuate died by the hundreds—that really didn't sit well with him, whether they were ordered to abandon Ingress or not.

He rose his arms, and they became twin energy guns. As he did, one of the soldiers, a decorated officer, rushed out and spread both hands, holding up his palms toward Jake's mech.

"Wait. Wait!" he yelled, his voice squeaking a little. "We can't have any fighting in here! The elevator's walls are only rated to take so much abuse. We can't fight you here."

"Surrender, then," Jake said. "Or I swear to God I'll blow you all apart, elevator be damned."

He was bluffing. At least, he was pretty sure he was bluffing. Either way, the soldiers threw their guns onto the floor and raised their hands in the air.

"Now bring this elevator back down to the planet," Jake commanded.

"What?" the officer said. "Are you crazy?"

"That's a separate issue. Our entire mission was to secure the elevator, and that's what's going to happen."

Another man stepped to the fore, alongside the officer. "Hi," he said, with a sarcastic little wave. "I'm this elevator's operator." The man pointed a thin finger at the doors where Jake had entered, where a fair amount of wind was whooshing through. "You just broke those. You do realize this is a *space* elevator, right? The doors failing to close properly might become a problem once we reach, you know, *space.*"

"That's why it just became your job to fix it," Jake ground out. "Better get to work. You don't have a lot of time."

Looking around, he realized the elevator didn't have enough room to accommodate all of the resistance army.

Making a snap decision, he contacted Councilman Pichenko to ask him to quickly find volunteers among the shuttle pilots willing to fly down to the planet's surface and pick up any Quatro in danger of being left behind.

CHAPTER 23

A Risky Play

Of the eight trainees Ash had been tasked with turning into MIMAS pilots, she'd identified three who seemed likely to stick with her once everything started falling apart aboard Valhalla. Of the other five, there was no one she felt sure enough about.

I'm not even completely sure about the three I've chosen. But the time for certainty was long past, and she needed to try to add as many assets as she could to the resistance's efforts.

That took her aback, for a moment—that she'd just thought of herself as a member of the resistance, rather than someone who was merely concerned for Jake and Marco.

I guess that is what actively working to undermine Darkstream makes me. Lying in her bed, waiting for the sedative she'd just popped to take effect, she shrugged. *Might as well embrace it.*

She'd instructed the three pilots she'd selected to meet her in a simulated version of Valhalla's Core.

As she walked across the airy, gleaming plaza that catered to the Steele System's richest people, she couldn't help thinking of the final test that Roach had subjected them to during training. It had involved Valhalla getting attacked by the Quatro, and it had been the job of the recruits who hadn't washed out yet to defend the station.

After they'd woken from the sim, it had occurred to Ash how outlandish the scenario had seemed. The idea of the Quatro somehow taking the space elevator to invade the station had seemed preposterous. And yet here they were, preparing for exactly that possibility.

She'd arranged to meet her pilots-in-training in the same green space where Jake had taken down a simulated Quatro, right before one of them had killed him—in the dream, anyway. But they'd all thought it was real, and Jake had sacrificed himself to save Marco.

Ash found the three trainees underneath an oak with branches that swept up toward the overhead display panels, which joined together seamlessly to give the illusion of a sapphire sky.

Maura Odell was one of the three she'd identified as likely to join her, which was lucky, given her proficiency. Ash was pleased that Benny Cho was another. Zed Gifford was a somewhat less fortunate addition. He was generally lackluster as a soldier, and Ash wasn't sure how he'd made it past training to be selected as one of the eight to form the next team of MIMAS pilots. She'd decided days ago that she had *no* desire to meet the trainees who'd washed out.

All three of the pilots-in-training before her had seemed pessimistic about Darkstream's chances of holding the station. Cho had even advocated surrendering, despite Ash's feigned discouragement of that conclusion.

"You must be wondering why I only asked you three to meet me here, and not the whole team," she said. They offered only blank expressions in response, so she continued. "To answer that, there's a lot to unpack. But first, let me give you access to a Red Company data dump, which I was strictly forbidden to share with anyone..."

It took her around a half hour to get them up to speed on her decision, as well as her reasons for it. For the most part, they responded with agreement—nodding heads, murmurs of assent.

For the most part.

Benny Cho only maintained his blank expression, barely blinking, even as she outlined her plan.

"Releasing Roach will cause the station to erupt in chaos," Ash said, "which will make it much easier for the resistance to come aboard and take control. Setting Roach free is a risky play, but I see it as much less risky than letting Darkstream marshal an orderly defense.

"I need you to meet me outside Alpha Quadrant at eighteen hundred hours, each of you inside your MIMAS. People on Valhalla are used to seeing the mechs walking around, by now, so you shouldn't raise too many eyebrows. Once we're all assembled, we'll bust Roach out together."

They all agreed to her plan—verbally, anyway. But Cho's eyes stayed blank and empty, in stark contrast with the set jaws of Odell and Gifford.

CHAPTER 24

Early Arrival

The space elevator arrived, but Lisa still wasn't confident she'd make it on. The mechanized army had pushed through the city streets with alarming speed, taking square after street after alley with a level of efficiency and coordination that the combined Darkstream and resistance armies simply weren't prepared for.

They'd retreated far enough that their backs were almost to the base of the elevator, and though her army had already begun loading aboard, the elevator only had one entrance. It would take time to get everyone on, and that was assuming the battle didn't leave the elevator with holes big enough to destroy its spaceworthiness.

"Tessa, how are things looking on your end?" Lisa asked over a two-way channel. She'd assigned Tessa to command the forces guarding the other side of the elevator.

"Not great," Tessa answered. "I give it twenty minutes before they break through to the elevator, and that's an optimistic projection."

Captain Arkady Black had been ordered to hold the city, and that's what he seemed determined to do, or at least to attempt. Lisa's respect for the man became less grudging with each passing minute. Black's suicidal last stand was the only reason the resistance army's mission was still possible.

She noticed shuttles approaching overhead; black specks that quickly became recognizable as spacecraft.

"Clear some space for those shuttles!" Lisa yelled over a wide channel, and the soldiers behind her responded just in time.

The shuttles swept overhead, following hair-raising trajectories that saw them barely clear the tops of some of the buildings. A couple of the shuttles performed landings that were closer to crashes, but all of the craft remained intact, proving that the pilots knew a lot more about flying than Lisa did.

"Everyone nearest the shuttles, pile on!" she ordered, speaking over a channel restricted only to members of the resistance. It felt odd to use the Darkstream soldiers as effective meat shields, when they'd been the enemy so recently.

Nothing about this war is conventional. And it seemed it would only get more unconventional as time went on.

At last, enough of her soldiers were on either the elevator or the shuttles for Lisa to feel justified in finding a place herself.

She encountered Jake and Rug at the elevator's doors, standing guard.

"Good thinking, calling for the shuttles from the refugee fleet," Lisa said, nodding at her childhood friend.

Jake nodded back in a way that looked weary even though it was the alien mech doing the nodding. As his gaze seemed to drift past Lisa, his entire body stiffened, and she turned to see what had caused the reaction.

Beth Arkanian was standing there, metal hands dangling at her sides. At least, Lisa assumed it was Arkanian. Marco piloted the only other MIMAS on Eresos that was still operational.

Jake seemed to have arrived at the same conclusion, though Lisa assumed he had means of identifying the MIMAS pilots that were superior to hers.

"What are you doing here?" he asked, his tone icy.

"Getting on," Arkanian said.

"You are, are you? So you're loyal enough to Darkstream to try your best to kill me, but not loyal enough to stay and die with them." If Jake hadn't been inside his mech, Lisa felt sure he would have spat.

"I want to see Ash," Arkanian said. "Do you really plan to try and stop me?"

"No," he said. "You're my teammate—at least, you were—and I'll honor that. I won't consign you to death, like you were so ready to do to me." With that, Jake stepped aside stiffly.

Arkanian walked onto the elevator, avoiding eye contact with everyone. She disappeared inside, to make herself as small and inconspicuous as she could while still inside a MIMAS, unless Lisa missed her guess.

Behind her, the thunder of war crescendoed. "We're the last ones," Lisa shouted over it. "Let's go."

Jake and Rug waited till she was aboard, and then they stepped on themselves. The elevator's operator stood next to the door with a meter-long tube of some sort of sealant, which he applied to the door's gaps while Jake held them closed.

"Hopefully that holds," the operator said, grimacing. "It's meant as an emergency measure, and you'll have to blow the doors open to get out again."

"Shouldn't be a problem," Jake said. "Now, get this thing off the ground."

Apparently, the operator didn't require further urging. *He's probably just as eager to leave Eresos as we are.*

Within thirty seconds, the elevator had begun its ascent, with the planet dropping away beneath them.

The inside of the elevator was crowded, but not unbearably so. Through a gap in the throng, Lisa watched Rug edge her way toward one of the floor-to-ceiling windows, which were made of silicon nitride—the same material used in beetle windows back on Alex.

Inching through the crowd, Lisa joined her old friend, who was resting on her haunches.

We've been through so much, she and I. Lisa placed a hand on the Quatro's enormous flank, and they looked out on the planet in silence, where so many suffered and died.

"Do you think they have any chance at all of survival?" Lisa asked.

"I do not," Rug said.

"You truly have no hope for them at all?"

In answer, the Quatro raised her gaze. Lisa followed it, inhaling sharply at what seemed like tens of thousands of meteorites streaking across the dawn-lit sky, hurtling toward the surface of Eresos. "Ravagers," she said, breathless.

"The Meddlers have arrived early," was all Rug said in reply.

CHAPTER 25

MIMAS Sim

Lisa became lost in foreboding thought as she watched the plummeting Ravagers, and she felt grateful when Rug finally broke their silence.

"Do you recall the secreted ship I told you about when we were still on Alex?"

"Of course. The one you concealed in the Outer Ring."

"Yes. There is something I did not tell you about that ship."

Lisa studied her friend, eyebrows raised. Her comprehension of Quatro body language still had a long way to go, but she thought that Rug looked sad. "What is it?"

"She was *my* ship. I was her captain. I volunteered to relinquish command of her, until such time that she might be needed."

"That...must have been hard."

"It was."

Footsteps sounded behind them, and Lisa turned to see Bob O'Toole approaching. He stepped between Lisa and Rug at the space elevator's windows, folding his hands behind his back and squinting out at the thousands of Ravagers screaming toward Eresos.

"You can say what you like about life on Alex," he said, "but we never got weather like this."

Lisa turned to face O'Toole. "You were just walking among the troops?"

"Uh, yes..."

"What's their mood? Are they anxious?"

O'Toole nodded with seeming reluctance. "They're worried one of the Ravagers will hit the elevator cable and snap it. Or that the mechanical army that chased us onto this thing will manage it."

Nodding, Lisa said, "The cables are strong. Hence their name, 'super-strong nanotethers.'" Despite her cavalier words, Lisa shared the fears of the others. She also knew there was nothing they could do about them but hope.

"Lisa," a second voice said from behind her, and she turned to behold Andy leaning on his crutches with his hands curled at his sides and his jaw set.

"Yes, Andy?"

"I'd like to talk."

"About what?"

Andy's gaze flitted to O'Toole, then back to Lisa just as quickly. "I'd like to talk in private."

O'Toole had adopted a concerned expression, which looked a little foreign on his face. Lisa tried to find the irony lurking beneath it, but couldn't.

"Don't you have family down there, son?" O'Toole said, sweeping his hand toward the planet below.

"I do," Andy said.

"Aren't you concerned for them?"

"No. They can burn."

Eyes widening, O'Toole turned back to the window, clasping his hands behind his back once more.

Meeting Andy's stare, Lisa tried to decide whether she should honor his request to speak in private. For one thing, she had a suspicion as to what their conversation would be about. For another, she wasn't sure there was any privacy to be had aboard the packed elevator at all.

Finally, he seemed to tire of her hesitation. "Do you love me?" he asked.

Lisa blinked. This was in the neighborhood of what she'd anticipated from him, but she hadn't expected him to be quite so direct. "Andy, I...I'm not sure what to say."

"Really," he said, his tone flat, and his body somehow going even more rigid. "We started something, back on Alex. Are you going to abandon it? After everything we've been through?"

"I'm not abandoning anything, least of all you. But I *would* remind you of a time when you abandoned me. We had some good times together, Andy, and then you cut me off completely."

He nodded. "I'm not denying that. But this, right now, this is different. Back then, that was just stupid dating games. It was before we survived together for months out on Alex. Before we embarked on a war against Darkstream. Everything is much realer, now."

Twisting her head for a glimpse of the Ravagers streaking through the sky, she returned her gaze to Andy. "It's basically the apocalypse, right now. This is no time to use the word love." With that, Lisa turned to find a place among her army.

"It's *exactly* the time!" Andy yelled after her.

"Now is the time to prepare for battle," she said without turning. With that, she began transmitting to Andy the MIMAS training sims that Marco had broken into for her. "Prepare well, Andy."

She reached a group of Quatro standing near a window, and she asked them to remain nearby and make sure no one tripped over her as she lay down to go lucid.

Minutes after taking a sedative, she found herself in the first sim, already inside a mech.

The experience was nothing short of astonishing.

CHAPTER 26

Worthy First
Targets

Ash walked her MIMAS outside of Alpha Quadrant and onto the giant plaza that formed Valhalla's core.

The scene she found there made her draw up short, retracting the fingers of both metal hands to rest against her wrists, revealing the rotary autocannons underneath.

Two of the three pilots with whom she'd shared her plan—Maura Odell and Zed Gifford—were outside of their mechs, kneeling on the ground with hands clamped to their heads.

Behind them, closest to Ash, stood the other six pilots of the team, all inside their machines. They'd arrayed themselves facing away from Alpha Quadrant, since that was the direction Ash was supposed to have come from...at least, according to the plan she'd fed them.

Their enhanced auditory sensors picked up the sound of her fingers clicking into place, and all six mechs turned, facing her and away from their pair of hostages. That might have given Gifford and Odell an opportunity to sprint toward their open mechs, except their captors were likely monitoring them through rear sensors.

"I see that you've deviated from my plan a bit," Ash said, her voice level.

"Wait," Benny Cho said. "What are you doing, coming *from* Alpha Quadrant? Didn't you want our help breaking Roach out?"

Ash shrugged, a gesture that was somewhat awkward to pull off inside a MIMAS, but she thought she managed it all right. "Oh. Well, see, *I* deviated from my plan a little, too."

"Why?"

"Because the purpose of my plan wasn't actually to get your help freeing Roach. I didn't need your help. The purpose was to find out which of you I could actually trust. And now I know."

"Take her down," Cho said.

Tremors reached Ash through the station's deck, and she leapt aside as all six mechs opened fire on where she'd been standing.

Their bullets hit Gabriel Roach instead, who was charging out of Alpha Quadrant. While the ordnance introduced a stutter to his step, it didn't slow him very much, and his right forearm sprouted a wicked, curved blade as he closed the distance with Benny Cho.

Cho extended both his bayonets—too late. Roach's sword found the mech's torso, exactly where Cho's unconscious form was nestled, and the blade impaled the MIMAS with ease.

The great machine slumped, lifeless, and Roach stepped clear of it, turning to face the closest opposing mech.

Four of the five remaining pilots confronting Roach trained their lasers on him, perhaps remembering the class when Ash had taught them that lasers had proved most effective against the alien-made mechs. The remaining MIMAS was otherwise occupied, though— with the high-velocity rounds with which Ash was perforating his mech.

Roach was too fast for the pilots to maintain a bead on him long enough for the lasers to do meaningful damage. Dancing backward, he widened his arms in a sweeping gesture. Almost too quickly to register, those arms became long-barreled energy cannons, which blasted holes clean through the mechs they were aimed at. Both of those mechs slumped to the deck, joining Cho.

The remaining three mechs, of which Orson Cole was one, raised their metal hands. "We surrender," Cole said, his voice laced with panic.

"Roach, *heel!*" Ash commanded.

Roach whirled toward one of the mechs, both arms becoming broadswords angled to slice through the MIMAS.

"*Roach!*"

He paused abruptly, his blades suspended inches from his target's neck and shoulders.

Ash wasted no time. "Out of your mechs," she ordered the surviving enemy pilots. Their backs popped open instantly, and the human pilots clambered out as soon as they emerged from their slumber, blinking groggily. Cole fell to his hands and knees.

Ash initiated a protocol she'd been given access to as the team's primary instructor. It allowed her to order the empty mechs to walk to a destination of her choosing. She instructed them to head for a location deep inside Omega Quadrant, which she'd identified in advance. It was one she would have full access to, but also hopefully the last place Darkstream would think to look in the chaos that would soon seize Valhalla Station.

The clatter of the mechs' footsteps as they jogged across the Core created a frenetic staccato.

"Get inside your mechs," she barked at Odell and Gifford, and they wasted no time in complying.

Next, she turned to Roach. He still had his broadswords extended...and now they were angled toward her.

"You shouldn't have released me," he rasped. "Don't you get it? I have no defenses against the whispers, anymore."

The whispers... "What are they telling you to do right now?"

"To kill," Roach said, taking a step toward her. "*Everything.*"

Ash stood her ground. "Then why don't you go take out your angst on Darkstream? If you're supposed to kill everything, they're worthy first targets, aren't they? I'm sure you're not very happy with them, and I doubt the whispers are, either."

Roach didn't budge, and for several long moments, Ash was convinced he would strike.

Abruptly, he charged across the Core, angling in a direction that should take him clear of the elevator.

Guilt racked her, and she realized this must be how Roach felt all the time. But she'd done what she needed to do. Wasn't that the essence of being a soldier?

CHAPTER 27

As Anticipated

Rather than a smaller chamber that let onto the station, the space elevator's airlock enveloped its entire structure. The elevator was designed to ascend directly into the airlock, which sealed underneath it.

This was meant as an extra failsafe, in case the elevator suffered a breach, but it now proved tactically useful to Lisa's invading army.

Under her orders, Jake and Rug had already positioned themselves directly opposite the entrance, which the operator had sealed shut.

They both directed energy cannons at the unbroken elevator wall, blasting it simultaneously with incredible force.

When the fire and smoke cleared, a yawning aperture had opened, and Jake and Rug were the first through.

Lisa followed directly after, with a pair of Quatro flanking her on both sides. As anticipated, the Darkstream military presence on this side of the elevator was sparse—the enemy had expected them to emerge through the actual doors.

It was a reasonable assumption, but it also happened to be wrong. Lisa raised her SL-17 to sight along its barrel at a baffled-looking soldier, planting a round in his neck and downing him. She tracked the assault rifle's sights across the vast expanse of Valhalla's Core, which she'd had Jake brief her on twice.

Another soldier was leaning out from the corner of what looked like a grocery store. Lisa's next round took her in the face, obliterating it and throwing her backward.

By the time the Darkstream forces in front of the elevator doors caught on to what had happened, Lisa's combined Quatro and human strike force had cleared out most of the resistance on this side.

Even so, the Darkstream reprisal was much swifter and fiercer than Lisa had expected—and it also involved far more soldiers.

"Take cover!" Lisa yelled as she ran for the hide her second target had been occupying. A bullet zipped in front of her face, but she suppressed the urge to recoil and continued sprinting forward.

Some of her soldiers outside the elevator would be forced to retreat back inside, she knew, creating a bottleneck. But they'd used the element of surprise to deploy as many soldiers as possible into the Core, and most of them had already found cover among the buildings and trees nearby.

Lisa soon had cause to swap out her magazine for a fresh one, and less than a minute later, she did it again. She'd set her assault rifle to fire in short bursts, and she spent each bullet judiciously, taking down five more hostiles.

They kept coming, though, pushing Lisa's position hard, along with most of her army's. She needed backup from inside the elevator, but the Darkstream soldiers were taking care to keep them pinned inside it, and Jake and Rug were too far away to blast open another exit.

A grenade skittered across the station's deck, coming to a stop near Lisa's feet. She hadn't seen where it had come from, but that didn't seem important right now, as she turned and sprinted along the building she'd chosen as her cover.

Diving for the rear corner, she made it around just as the grenade was going off. The ground shook, and she was almost knocked her off her feet.

Peering around the building, Lisa saw that her attackers hadn't relied solely on the grenade. One of them was charging through the dissipating smoke, and she put a round in the center of his forehead, but more were coming behind.

Maybe they've identified me as the commander.

Probably it had been stupid for her to deploy from the elevator so early, but she'd already persuaded herself that their only chance of winning this war involved taking big risks, and seeing her lead from the front *had* boosted morale among her soldiers.

Getting killed will devastate morale. Yet she saw no avenue of escape. Behind her was an open area that stretched too far for her to cross in time.

There was nothing for it but to face her attackers head-on. She dropped to one knee, pressing herself against the rear of the building and angling her gun upward.

Two men and two women rushed around the corner. Lisa took down one of the former and one of the latter, but the remaining pair both spread out and drew beads on her.

I'm dead.

The sharp staccato of heavy machine gun fire sounded, mowing down the soldier nearest the building, who Lisa had been aiming at. She rolled sideways, shifting targets and planting a round into a gap in the remaining hostile's combat armor, at the top of his thigh.

His gun went off as he fell, but the shot went high, scoring the building a couple feet above Lisa's head. She strode forward and shot him in the face. Then she turned to take in her rescuer.

It was a MIMAS mech, its face and torso covered in yellow whorls, and Lisa recognized it as the one piloted by Ash Sweeney.

"Where's Beth?" the mech pilot asked, not wasting time on formalities.

"Pinned inside the elevator."

Nodding, Ash dashed around the building to join the fight.

Two other mechs had shown up with Ash, and their arrival singlehandedly turned the tide of the battle. Within twenty minutes, the last Darkstream soldiers had died, fled, or been captured.

Within seconds of that, Ash Sweeney and Beth Arkanian were out of their mechs, wrapped in a tight embrace as they shared a passionate kiss.

Jake approached Lisa from a cluster of buildings nearby, where she gathered there'd been a pitched firefight. "That'll be far from the only station defenders. The ones that ran will marshal more of the garrison."

"You're right. We need to prioritize taking a landing bay. Once we have the soldiers your shuttles picked up, we should be able to secure the rest of the station with minimal casualties."

Nodding, Jake said, "We'd better get moving."

CHAPTER 28

Valhalla's Defensive Arsenal

"How you holding up, Clutch?"

Jake glanced across the entrance to Landing Bay Theta, where Marco's MIMAS was crouched, ducking out periodically to fire on the Darkstream soldiers. They were mounting a much fiercer defense of the landing bay than anyone had expected.

Inside his own mech, Jake smiled. Marco could already see how he was holding up, but he knew that wasn't the actual point of the question.

The point was to use his old nickname. His Oneiri nickname.

"Hanging in there, Spirit. You?"

"I say we charge these corporate bootlickers. Draw their fire, return some suppressive fire of our own, and let our people pour in behind us. We'll have the landing bay in no time."

Jake considered the suggestion for a moment. It was risky, but risky was exactly what they needed right now.

"All right. Let's try to lay off the rockets—the landing bay won't be of much use to us if we blow a hole in the side of the station."

"Roger that. Let's do this."

They charged in as one, Marco's rotary autocannons firing at full bore while Jake unleashed thin rods of light—pinpoint laser strikes meant to neutralize the hostiles without doing too much damage to the station itself.

Behind, Quatro poured into the landing bay. The first two squads of aliens were armed, and they laid down suppressive fire of their own. That allowed dozens more unarmed Quatro to flood in, charging along the sides of the landing bay and clearing out the human soldiers crouching behind cover. The effort ended in several dead aliens, but the Quatro seemed to recognize the urgency of the day, and they didn't shy away from kamikaze tactics whenever the situation called for it.

They've been downtrodden for too long—by the ones they call the Meddlers and by humans, too. They've had enough.

Within minutes they'd secured the area, after a handful of soldiers threw down their weapons, surrendering in time to save themselves.

The resistance leaders had all agreed that anyone surrendering would be granted whatever asylum was still available to them in the Steele System. Jake ordered his soldiers to take their guns, and they bound them hand and foot, but they were permitted to live.

Marco was already out of his mech and running for the landing bay's compact control room, which sat in the corner that was farthest from the large airlock. For his part, Jake busied himself with contacting Councilman Pichenko and letting him know that a landing bay had been secured and that the shuttles were cleared to enter.

"Uh, Jake?" It was Marco, subvocalizing.

"What's up?"

"I had a glance at the station's sensor data from the last couple hours...you're not going to like this. Every last UHF warship Darkstream has at its disposal has turned toward us and is headed our way. The *Javelin's* already here, but it seems to be waiting for more ships to arrive before engaging."

Jake's stomach turned to ice, and the mech dream treated him to a mounting drumbeat. He turned to face the control room, and his eyes met Marco's through the glass. Enhanced visual sensors told him that the other pilot's eyes were wide.

"Can we use the station's guns against the ships?" Jake asked.

After a long pause, Marco said, "Maybe. But it would involve hacking into Valhalla's weapon systems and convincing the computer to target the warships as enemies. That's no easy feat, especially since we have little more than an hour to do it."

"We have to try. And we'd better finish taking the station before the warships get here, too. Otherwise, some Darkstream tech can just switch the targeting back. We'll need all our mechs outside, engaging those ships."

Marco swallowed visibly. "I know the MIMAS mechs are *rated* for space combat, but the capability's never been tested—"

"It has, actually. By me."

Nodding, Marco said, "All right, then. In order to mess with the defensive arsenal's targeting, we need to take the station's control center. Fast."

"Agreed. Maybe we can lower the station's temperature while we're there. That'll make the Quatro's superconducting ability a lot more powerful."

Pichenko contacted Jake, then, interrupting their conversation.

"Councilman. What can I do for you?"

"Jake, a shuttle full of Quatro was just shot down by one of Valhalla's turrets. The guns must have been reprogrammed to recognize us as hostile."

That made Jake curse. The station's weapons weren't supposed to target any human ships.

"Councilman, tell the pilots to back off until I give the go-ahead," Jake said. He returned his gaze to Marco, switching back to their two-way channel. "I just received word that Valhalla's weapons are targeting our shuttles. The need to take the control center just became even greater. Let's move."

Jake turned to deliver orders to his remaining force in the landing bay.

Hopefully Lisa and Ash are making out better than we are.

CHAPTER 29

Fight for It

Except for Arkanian and Sweeney, who were both inside their mechs, Lisa had no backup as she jogged through the corridors of Omega Quadrant, assault rifle at the ready.

There was Andy, of course—currently being carried in Arkanian's metal arms—though sadly, Lisa couldn't count him as meaningful support.

Not yet, anyway.

"How are you doing, Andy?"

He sniffed. "Other than being carried by a glorified tin can, I'm fine."

But something about Andy's tone was different. Lisa thought she detected a note of hope, where none had been before.

It turned out that after Lisa had walked away from him on the space elevator, Andy had also taken advantage of the downtime to undergo the MIMAS training sims. Now, they were headed to an underused cargo hold where three empty mechs were waiting, vacant and ready for new pilots.

Resistance was sparse in the Omega Quadrant, which was a little surprising, given this was the quadrant where Darkstream housed most of its military personnel.

They don't think there's much here worth protecting. And they'd be right, if it wasn't for Ash.

They avoided the quadrant's weapons lockers, as well as any areas that Beth and Ash warned were likely to contain troves of sensitive data. Those places likely *would* be heavily guarded, which would slow them down at best.

At last, they arrived at the cargo hold. Ash punched in her access code, which still worked, thankfully. It seemed no one had thought to revoke her access during the chaos of the invasion.

Lisa supposed they could have simply blown open the cargo hold if need be, but that would have risked structural damage to the station while likely drawing unwanted attention.

She'd piloted MIMAS mechs during the handful of training sims she'd had time to undergo, but nothing in real life was ever quite like it was in the dream. Why that was, she still hadn't figured out, since the simulations generated by lucid were essentially perfect.

Maybe memory gets in the way of the mind's acceptance of the dream.

Whatever the reason, chills went up her spine as she approached one of the three real-life mechs, in a way that hadn't occurred when she'd beheld the MIMAS simulacra.

"I've granted your implant exclusive access to the MIMAS in front of you," Sweeney said. "Go ahead. Open it up."

Lisa willed the metal giant to open to her, just as she had countless times inside the training sims. It did, a portion of its back popping out to lower and become a ramp for her to climb. She swallowed the required sedative, which Arkanian had already supplied her with, and then she clambered into the machine.

She felt the mech close around her, enveloping her snugly. The constriction combined with the total darkness to induce a brief wave of claustrophobia, but that passed as the mech dream took her and she *became* the mech.

Its arms were her arms—its strength her strength. Even its weapons felt like natural extensions, and she noticed that inside the mech dream, that didn't feel odd at all. On the contrary, it seemed totally natural. And why shouldn't it? Lucid had the ability to tweak one's consciousness, so why not tweak it in a direction that made her a better pilot?

"Walk toward me," Sweeney said. "I want to make sure everything's properly calibrated."

Lisa took a step forward, and when she did, she felt the storeroom tremble around her. A pile of boxes shifted nearby, then toppled over.

The sense of power, combined with the knowledge that this was real life and not lucid, was almost overwhelming. She yearned to fight something—to kill an enemy. That surprised her, since she didn't condone violence for violence's sake. This urge to find an enemy just so she could kill it...

Makes me realize how hard Jake has it, piloting a machine that regularly urges him to kill. And how hard Roach had it.

According to Ash, Roach was still out there somewhere. Still on this station, a living weapon that outmatched even the one Lisa had just taken control of.

I can't let this thing make me rash. MIMAS pilots aren't invincible. That's a lesson that's been learned the hard way, several times over.

"Me next," Andy said, with more excitement than Lisa had ever heard from him.

Arkanian carried him to one of the other mechs, and a silent command caused it to lower its rear ramp to admit him.

The former Oneiri pilot deposited Andy inside the tough fabric cocoon, and Andy held himself there with his arms.

The MIMAS sealed around him.

Moments later, the mech came to life, turning toward Lisa and raising its arms.

From inside the mech—from inside the dream—came Andy's voice.

"This...this is incredible," he said. If Lisa hadn't known better, she would have said he sounded choked up. "I think I just got my life back."

"You have it for now," Sweeney said, her tone flat as she turned toward the exit. "If you want to hold on to what you've gained for more than a few hours, you're going to have to fight for it."

CHAPTER 30

Oneiri Team

Eager to end the battle for the control room quickly, Jake charged straight into the barricades the Darkstream soldiers were taking cover behind.

Though the barricades folded out from the walls, they were titanium-plated, and fairly sturdy. Still, they weren't built to withstand the might of an alien mech.

The barriers buckled under Jake's weight, and he made short work of the surviving soldiers. One took a hastily morphed blade through the neck, and another through the stomach. Jake didn't have time to shake them free as he spun, heavy guns sprouting from his shoulders to take down the remaining three soldiers.

It was a gruesome affair, and as the dead soldiers slid from his retracting blades, Jake winced inwardly at how little chance unarmored humans stood against mechs. No matter what followed today, the past year had forever changed the way wars were waged. If humanity couldn't adapt in time, they would surely die out.

Judging by the way the Darkstream soldiers had chosen to organize their defense of the primary control room, Darkstream hadn't yet been pushed to a scorched earth policy, or whatever the space-based equivalent would be. They'd chosen not to do their fighting from inside the control room itself, and the reason was obvious: they recognized its importance and didn't want it damaged.

When Jake climbed out of his mech to enter what was effectively the station's brain, he found it empty. The technical personnel had apparently been evacuated well before the battle, probably as a safeguard against the control room getting compromised.

That probably means this is going to be every bit as difficult as Marco thinks. If Darkstream had been prepared to abandon the control room, it confirmed that the security measures against tampering would be robust. That wasn't entirely surprising, but it could mean the difference between winning and losing in the coming battle against the warships.

"Get to work, Spirit," Jake said. "I need the station's turrets to identify the warships as enemies. And lowering the temperature for the Quatro will only be effective if we do it soon."

Marco looked at him with what closely resembled a glare. "Clutch, hacking the defensive arsenal is going to be difficult enough—you can't just tell me to hack a second unfamiliar system at the same time and expect results within a meaningful timeframe!"

Smiling, Jake walked over to his fellow mech pilot and slapped him on the shoulder. "No problem, Spirit. We'll just lose, then. No big deal. Don't worry about it—no one will blame you."

He turned away, leaving Marco wearing an expression that combined confusion and anger in equal measure.

Jake left the control room to find five MIMAS mechs approaching down the corridor. He was about to scramble inside his own machine when he recognized two of the mechs as Ash's and Beth's. He strode out to meet them.

His practiced eye told him that one of the mechs was unpiloted—it was operating under a basic tag-along command.

"Who's inside those?" he asked, nodding at the two new mechs that did have pilots.

"It's me," said Lisa. "And that's Andy." The MIMAS' giant hand gestured at the other mech.

Andy remained silent, which made Jake reflect that now there were two mech pilots with whom relations were strained—he still didn't feel comfortable around Beth, either, given that she'd recently tried to kill him. *But I need to use every asset available to me.*

The realization that he was now thinking of his former teammates as "assets" made him feel too much like Bronson, and he had to suppress a shudder. Turning back to Ash, he said, "You recruited two other pilots as well, didn't you? Where are they?"

"Sato sent them with Rug to clear out Alpha Quadrant."

Jake nodded. "Are we putting Notaras inside the extra mech?"

"Not so much," Lisa answered. "She said something along the lines of 'I'd rather be gunned down inside my own body, thank you very much.'"

Tilting his head to one side, Jake decided not to comment on that notion. He immediately saw a couple things wrong with it, but it wasn't worth arguing about right now.

"Darkstream's battle group is going to get here any minute," he said. "We need to get to Landing Bay Theta ASAP. I've already secured it, and as far as I know, we still control it. I'll make sure of that while we're en route."

"If Darkstream's retaken it, we'll just take it back," Lisa said.

"Exactly. I need you to tell Rug to order the new pilots to meet us there. We'll need every mech we have in the battle against the warships."

Other than glimpses of frightened civilians, either hiding from the mechs or fleeing, the trip to Landing Bay Theta was totally uneventful.

That made sense to Jake. Watching five MIMAS mechs and one alien mech charging full bore across the space station likely didn't do much for the enemy soldiers' fighting spirit. Either way, Jake didn't see any sign of hostiles.

I guess they've given up the Core. He knew there were still pockets of defenders entrenched in the quadrants, but the mechs' path across the center of the station was clear. Rug and Tessa probably had a lot to do with that—they each commanded a separate force, and were keeping the remaining defenders busy in the Alpha and Epsilon Quadrants.

When they arrived at the landing bay, the other two MIMAS mechs were already there. "This is Maura Odell and Zed Gifford," Ash said.

Jake nodded. "I'm Jake Price, and this is Lisa Sato, Andy Miller, and..." He cleared his throat. "And Beth Arkanian."

By her stiff body language, Jake could tell that Beth was feeling just as awkward as he was. "Jake," she said softly. "I'm sorry, okay? I was wrong to side with Darkstream against you. It's just that I knew they had Ash, and all I could think about was her safety."

"That's a pretty convenient thing for you to say," Jake said.

Inclining her head, Beth said, "I know. But it's all I have for you. Besides, you *need* me."

"You're right. I do need you. We all do." He sighed. "We'll figure out the other stuff after all this is over. Today is about survival—about pulling out of this mess as best we can." He looked around at each of the mechs before him. "All I know is, it looks like Oneiri Team is back. Let's keep it that way."

CHAPTER 31

Make It Happen

Jake rocketed out of the airlock with six MIMAS mechs at his back.

"Now!" he yelled, and all seven mechs split off from each other, each adopting a different trajectory. There was no pattern to their movements, and to make them as difficult to hit as possible, Jake had ordered them to be ready to randomize their movements at a moment's notice.

Essentially, this was guns-D in zero gravity—the type of maneuver last pulled off by the *Providence*'s Condor fighter pilots, as far as anyone in the Steele System knew.

Unlike those Condor pilots, each MIMAS had a tactical display more immersive than anything that had preceded it, which allowed the pilots much more responsiveness. They didn't just see threats—they *felt* them, with a jolt of fear and instinct that carried a directional element. Such were the advantages provided by the mech dream.

The warship closest to the newly reformed Oneiri team, a destroyer, loosed an opening salvo, with two Banshee missiles targeting each mech.

They're testing us. Seeing how we react. The destroyer was the *Javelin*, piloted by Bronson, who knew Jake had experience with space combat from when they'd fought a host of robots together out in the Belt.

But he's banking on my pilots not having any experience.

And the man was right to do so. Outside sims, Oneiri had never battled with their mechs in space.

Worse, half of the team was now comprised of rookies, which was underscored when the second missile targeting Zed Gifford connected squarely with his lower torso.

"Gifford," Jake barked over the team-wide channel. "Evasive maneuvers!"

Gifford was changing his position relative to the destroyer, but his course took the form of a spiral that looked as awkward as it was predictable. "Sir, the blast affected my thrusters!"

Jake was far from an officer, but he decided now wasn't the time to correct Gifford about addressing him as "sir." The *Javelin* had opened fire with kinetic impactors, bisecting Gifford's wild circling in a way that was sure to hit him if he didn't tighten up. "Your other thrusters are fully operational," Jake said. "You need to compensate—"

It was too late. Kinetic impactors slammed into Gifford's MIMAS, taking out still more thrusters, and seconds later more rounds hit him, perforating the mech worse than swiss cheese.

Gifford's vitals went black, and he didn't respond to further transmissions. The mech's thrusters deactivated, giving the final sign that the MIMAS had become nothing more than scrap floating through space.

Cursing, Jake rocketed toward the destroyer to exact some revenge. Oneiri Team had just reformed, and already Bronson had taken one of their members from them, knocking them down to seven including Marco.

Beyond the *Javelin,* the system's only missile cruiser was maneuvering to get into position to start firing on Oneiri. Apparently Bronson noticed that too, as the destroyer went fully on the offense, sending a cloud of missiles at Jake while attempting to hit him with lasers.

Bronson remembers exactly what my mech is capable of doing to his ship.

Jake reversed thrust abruptly, sending thin energy bolts to meet the missiles before they could lay him open.

Then the missile cruiser, which Jake knew as the *Alexander*—its name had been changed to that when the planet, Alexandria, had received its name—moved into position and loosed two dozen Banshees straight at Jake.

They know that if they take me out, we'll fall apart. Jake wasn't one to overestimate his own importance, but he knew it was true. He was the only one with space combat experience, and without the benefit of his orders, the others would likely fall. Plus he was now Oneiri's de facto leader, and his mech was by far the most powerful.

But he refused to let the attack stoke his rage to the point of clouding his judgment. Instead, he rallied himself, accelerating backward and picking off each rocket while conserving as much energy as possible.

He opened up a channel with Marco, whose likeness the mech dream inserted into the space before him, which was a bit jarring. "Spirit, why aren't the station's defense systems targeting these warships?"

With a bitter chuckle, Marco said, "I told you how long this would take. It just can't be done that fast."

"Marco," Jake spat, dropping his teammate's nickname, "your attitude right now is disgusting. What has being part of Oneiri taught us about facing impossible odds? Did it teach us to just lay down and die? Is that what you got from it?"

Radio silence followed Jake's words.

"We've already lost a pilot," he went on. "Within the first two minutes. We're overpowered by just two ships, and more are on the way. *One of our teammates is already dead!*"

"All right," Marco said tersely. "All right!"

"Make it happen," Jake snapped. "*Now.*" He cut off the transmission, and Marco vanished.

At a glance, Jake saw from the data breakdown of his omni-directional tactical display that a destroyer was about to join the battle, with two corvettes due to arrive fifteen minutes behind it.

CHAPTER 32

Miracle Timing

"We need to start hitting back," Jake said over the team-wide. "Hard."

"Difficult to do without the station's turrets backing us up," Ash said.

"I know." Jake racked his brain for the optimal tactics for this situation. It was true that he had space combat experience, but outside of training and sims, he had zero experience with commanding a *squad* of mechs in space.

"Odell, Sato, and Miller, you provide missile defense for Sweeney and Arkanian as they focus fire on that missile cruiser. It's causing us the most grief right now."

"What will you do?" Andy said, and his tone had some bite.

"I'm taking on the destroyer that just showed up."

The alien mech did everything it could to communicate the danger involved as he hurtled toward the newly arrived destroyer. Great, glowing rents appeared in the fabric of space, flashing with the red of hellfire. Insects covered him, their spindly limbs skittering over his skin, and together they writhed like a living coat. The discordant violin note he'd first heard out in the Belt rose sharply until it was earsplitting.

But he was committed, even as the destroyer, called the *McDougal*, spat kinetic impactors at his mech, following up with lasers that played across empty space, trying to get a fix on him.

Jake wouldn't grant them that, nor would he provide an easy target for the kinetic impactors screaming his way, or the missiles that came soon after.

He hurled energy bolt after energy bolt at the missiles, thanking God for the alien mech's advanced targeting and predictive AI. Unlike the missiles, the energy blasts lacked the ability to alter their course after being fired, so Jake had to use everything at his disposal to anticipate where the missiles would be.

It wasn't long before the *Alexander* seemed to take notice of how close Jake was getting to the *McDougal* and sent an immense salvo of missiles his way. The destroyer sent its own barrage, and Jake knew immediately that he wouldn't be able to pick them all off with his energy guns.

So he lowered his guns and waited, continuing his course toward the destroyer but otherwise doing nothing to deal with the ordnance hurtling toward him.

At the last second, he repeated a trick he'd picked up in the Belt. Thin spikes exploded from all over his body, but this time they flew through space to intercept the missiles, whereas before they'd remained attached to him, each impaling a Ravager.

Within the space of twenty seconds, every missile was neutralized. The maneuver had cost Jake some of his mass, but he knew he could reclaim it, given access to the correct raw materials.

But how in Sol did I do that? He'd hoped the move would be possible, but he hadn't been sure. High-risk situations often seemed to bring out capabilities in the alien mech that he'd known nothing about.

If we merge, you will have ready access to them all, the whispers told him, but Jake ignored them as he closed with the *McDougal*, the bullets from the point defense system smacking against him like gnats.

Just before he landed, he sent an enormous energy blast at the hull, blowing open a hole wide enough for him to pass through.

He found himself inside a mid-size cargo hold filled with towering stacks of metal crates. Knowing it wouldn't be long before damage control teams arrived with marine escorts to seal the breach, he sprinted toward the exit, prying the doors open with wedge-shaped appendages he'd grown for the job.

Marines were already in the corridor outside, and Jake made short work of them with high-velocity rounds.

His journey toward the destroyer's CIC went similarly. It reminded him of how depressingly easy it had been when he'd stolen the alien mech from the *Javelin*'s shuttle bay. Except, his success today was even more disproportionate. Now that he was inside the ship itself, there was almost nothing the *McDougal*'s defenders could do to stop him. They had no mechs of their own, and no tanks. Jake reached the CIC with ease, blasting apart the security door meant to protect the captain and CIC crew from intruders.

Inside, almost all of the faces of the *McDougal*'s officers had gone white, and those that hadn't shone with sweat.

All except the captain, Joseph Baird. He appraised Jake coolly from the captain's chair, eyebrows arched.

"You're at my mercy," Jake told them all. "I wield the power to rip this ship apart from the inside. But I won't do that if you do exactly as I say."

"I know you, boy," Captain Baird said, sneering. "Bronson told me all about you, and I even came across you a few times during your training. You're a lot of things, but you wouldn't kill the crew of a ship you've taken hostage. You—"

Jake planted a high-velocity round inside the captain's skull, causing it to rupture like an overripe melon and spraying his Tactical and Coms officers with brains and blood. They recoiled, raising their arms and wincing.

Shifting the gun toward the Tactical officer—a stooped, graying woman with red and pink speckled across her face—Jake said, "Commander Stephanie Yates, is that correct?"

"That's right," she said, her voice shaking only slightly.

"You've just been given command of this ship. Are you willing to do as I say, or do I need to give the command to someone else?"

"I'll do it."

Jake nodded. "Hit the *Alexander* with twenty Banshees and follow up with kinetic impactors until she's neutralized." Turning to the sensor operator, Jake said, "Put up a tactical display showing the battle."

The sensor operator said nothing, but he did as Jake told him. A brief study of the viewscreen told him what he wanted to know: Marco had finally managed to compromise the safeguards for Valhalla's defensive arsenal. The station turrets were already firing on the *Javelin* and the *Alexander.*

The destroyer shook. "What was that?" Jake barked.

"Valhalla's turrets," the sensor operator said. "They're firing on us, too."

"Damn it," Jake spat, opening up a two-way channel with Marco. "Spirit, I need you to stop the turrets from firing on the *McDougal.*"

"Are you serious? I just finished convincing them that every warship it sees is an enemy! Now I have to persuade them that one of them is on our side after all?"

"That's right," Jake said.

"And what timeline would you like *this* miracle to adhere to?"

"Five minutes ago would be ideal."

CHAPTER 33

Gated Community

Tessa popped over a low garden wall, sent an uncontrolled burst in the direction of the Darkstream soldiers entrenched around the entrance to the gated community, and then ducked back down in time to avoid the hail of bullets the enemy soldiers sent her way in return.

She poked over the wall to fire again, but this time her SL-17 jammed, and she cursed, crouching to dismantle the weapon on the grass as quickly as possible.

The force she commanded had hit an impasse, unable to push forward with the numbers left to them after the constant fighting they'd endured on their way across the Core and into Epsilon Quadrant.

If she'd had more human soldiers, she might have been having more success—the cover available in this position was too squat and cramped to allow Quatro to push forward without taking unacceptable losses. Hers was the most advanced position, and the pressure the enemy soldiers was putting on her prevented her from retreating to join the Quatro in position around the homes behind her.

There's something inside that gated community. Something they're awfully eager to prevent us from accessing.

Tessa knew Darkstream. She didn't just know their tactics; she knew how to read them, too. As she encountered more and more push-back during her advance into the Epsilon Quadrant, she'd become increasingly sure: there was something here that would prove decisive in the conflict being waged between the resistance and the corporation.

Epsilon was home not only to Valhalla Station's famous Endless Beach, but also its most affluent residents. Mostly Darkstream executives.

Tessa highly doubted the company would keep sensitive data here, or valuable weaponry. Not so close to its top executives' homes.

No, she knew what she expected to find here: the members of the board of directors, huddled inside their homes within Valhalla's most sumptuous gated community.

Of course. Where else would they hide but the place they've always felt safest, the place where they were always able to keep the rabble out?

"The rabble's come for you," Tessa muttered as she clicked the last part of her assault rifle into place, reloaded, and bobbed over the garden wall to fire again.

"Tessa Notaras." It was Rug, coming in over a two-way channel.

Tessa crouched back down, mentally sweeping aside an alert from her implant that told her the ambient temperature was dropping steadily. "Rug. Do you have some good news for me?"

She'd contacted the Quatro twenty minutes ago, about the possibility of sending more troops her way. At the time, nobody had considered it worthwhile to fight through the station's residential areas.

"I do. Marco Gonzalez has succeeded in hacking the station's defensive arsenal. In doing so, he stopped them from targeting the shuttles carrying our reinforcements."

"How many of them can you send me?"

"Twenty Quatro. Most of them armed."

Tessa resisted the urge to curse again. It wasn't nearly as many as she would have liked—apparently, her allies still weren't convinced about what she was doing. But Tessa was sure that the mere fact that Epsilon was so heavily guarded meant it was worth attacking.

"At least most are armed, I guess," Tessa said. "Send them my way. I'll do my best to hold on till they get here."

"They are already en route."

The transmission ended, and Tessa grimaced. She'd been about to ask Rug if she knew anything about the plummeting temperature. *Hopefully the life support systems aren't failing on us.* In the meantime, her jumpsuit would keep her warm.

She did her best to keep up the pressure on the enemy soldiers, to prevent them from swarming her and ending her little campaign before it harvested the fruit she knew awaited it.

She'd been doing a lot of thinking, lately—about her future. Tessa wasn't young by any stretch, but she would have given herself ten more good fighting years, and two or three decades of life beyond that, given current technology.

Her ideas about where she'd likely end up spending those years had started to solidify on the space elevator, while she watched the end of Eresos take shape.

The end of the entire Steele System, probably.

If this system was going down, then survival meant fleeing from it.

She'd spent a lot of time with the Quatro, enough to know how unlikely it was that they'd be willing to return to what they called their Home Systems. That meant there was only one safe haven left to any Steele System refugees:

The Milky Way.

Whether humanity's home galaxy was actually a safe haven depended on several factors, especially for Tessa. What would facing human society mean for her, at whose feet many people laid the hundreds of thousands of deaths that had resulted from the failure of dark tech? She'd been the one to let the Ixan, Ochrim, access the master control for every warship's wormhole generator, and in doing so, she'd inadvertently signed the death warrants of all those military men and women.

Of course, whether she'd face consequences for that depended on whether humanity survived in any form back in the Milky Way. The year Darkstream had fled the galaxy, victory over the Ixa had seemed far from likely. Just a few months before the company's departure, the Ixa had devoured the Coreopsis System with thousands of advanced warships.

As Tessa continued to fire on the Darkstream soldiers guarding the gated community before her, she couldn't decide which would be worse for her: returning to find the Ixa had won the war, or that humanity had.

It didn't matter. Today had involved the drawn-out process of realizing what had become their only option: they *had* to risk a return to the Milky Way, and it wasn't reasonable for her to impede that effort because of her own past. For her friends—her brothers- and sisters-in-arms—she would accept whatever awaited her.

When she ducked down after delivering her latest salvo, pressing her back to the garden wall, she saw signs that the Quatro reinforcements had arrived—large forms flitting between structures, shadows flickering behind vine-covered trellis walls.

Without warning, a fifty-strong Quatro force charged toward the gated community, around a third of them armed.

"Stop!" Tessa yelled. "Go back!" The Quatro charge amounted to pointless suicide, but her warning was lost in the roar of gunfire as every Darkstream soldier opened up on the aliens.

None of them seemed affected by the volley, though, and Tessa blinked in confusion. A soft clattering sound reached her ears, and suddenly, she realized what it was: the bullets the enemy soldiers had fired were falling uselessly to the ground.

She got it, then. The station's falling temperature was not an accident. It had been engineered, to grant the Quatro full use of their fullerene-laced brains.

Poking her head over the garden wall, Tessa was just in time to watch as most of the Darkstream soldiers were thrown forcefully against the three-meter brick wall surrounding the gated community. Other enemy combatants had their guns wrenched from their grasps by the same invisible force, and a couple even had their skulls caved in with their own weapons.

Within seconds, it was over. Tessa stood, then, walking calmly toward the gate, which was dragged aside by the same force that had taken care of the soldiers.

The Quatro fell in around her. "Post a guard at the gate to make sure no one escapes," she barked at the Quatro she'd designated as her second-in-command. "Send two parties along the walls to find any other exits and secure them. I want everyone else searching the homes."

It didn't take long to find what she was looking for. Huddled in the parlor room of the largest mansion, they found all six members of the Darkstream board of directors.

Tessa smiled, taking a moment to enjoy their expressions, which ranged from fear to indigestion.

"If you like living," she told them, "you'll order your warships to stand down. All of them."

CHAPTER 34

We Aren't
Darkstream

Lisa breathed a sigh of relief as her metal feet connected with the deck of Landing Bay Theta. Fighting in zero-G had been far more disorienting than first entering the MIMAS had been—that said, the latter had felt so natural it was almost scary.

"Good work, Oneiri Team," Jake said. "I know we've lost a teammate already, but we honored Gifford's death by *winning*. I like to think he'd appreciate that."

"Plus, things could have been a lot worse," Ash chimed in.

"They *are* a lot worse," said a voice with a Hispanic accent, and they all turned to find Marco, inside his mech again, standing at the landing bay's entrance.

"What are you talking about?" Jake asked.

"Tens of thousands of ships—I have to assume they're warships, but they're like none I've ever seen before. They just appeared all along the Outer Ring of the Steele System."

"They have us surrounded?"

"I mean, yes," Marco said. "But I'd say the more relevant detail is how many of them there are. Tens of thousands, Jake. I don't think a battle group of rusty old UHF ships is going to do much against that, even backed up by a few spacefaring mechs."

"What are they doing now?" Lisa asked.

"Just sitting there, or at least they were three hours ago, which is how long light takes to reach us from out there. It's like they're waiting for something."

Lisa's heartbeat accelerated, and the mech dream made her peripheral vision pulse. She still hadn't gotten used to the way it turned her emotions into phenomena that warped reality. "They could be headed for us right now."

Jake nodded. "The fighting on Valhalla is basically over. A handful of Darkstream soldiers ignored the board's command to surrender, but they're mostly keeping to themselves. We should call everyone here and decide our next moves."

"Can we trust the Darkstream warships not to strand us here?" Lisa asked, gesturing with a metal hand toward the airlock.

"Well, they seem to listen to the board, and it's in the board's best interest to cooperate with us."

"Still..." Lisa shook her head. "All those enemy warships could easily cause the captains to panic and run."

"You're right. For now, I'll have Rug assign a squad of Quatro to every ship, to keep an eye on the CIC crews. Later, we'll divide the Quatro more or less evenly across the entire battle group. "

It took twenty minutes for most of the resistance leaders to assemble in Landing Bay Theta. Tessa was among them, and she had the Darkstream board of directors in tow. They didn't look very happy, and their designer clothes looked strange among the mechs, the Quatro, and the handful of militia members left over from Alex.

Oneiri Team formed a circle with their mechs, then each pilot exited—except for Ash, who was still recovering from getting impaled by Roach outside Vanguard. Lisa blinked groggily as she climbed down the ramp formed by her MIMAS' back, and her forearm stung a little. When she reached the ground, she studied the spot where the needle had punctured her wrist to inject the sedative's antagonist.

"So," Jake said, studying the six members of the board with an expression that bordered on contempt. "Have you figured out how you're going to extract a profit from the mess you've created?"

Suzanne Defleur, who was chairperson of the Darkstream board of directors, returned Jake's gaze through silver wisps of hair that hung over her face, having sprung free from her otherwise elaborate hairdo. Lisa had once had a lot of respect for Defleur. *Once.*

"We've failed," she said, and she actually sounded contrite. Lisa was nowhere near ready to accept anything Defleur said or did as authentic, but maybe this was a good sign. "There isn't much else to be said on the topic. Like Icarus, we reached too far, and now we burn for it."

Lisa shook her head. "There's something you're not telling us."

Defleur returned her glare wearing a blank expression, and the rest of the board behaved similarly.

Masterful acting. Whatever they were hiding, it had to be something big. Else, they wouldn't be putting this much effort into concealing it. Lisa doubted the board members were used to putting this much effort into anything.

"You're probably right, Lisa," Jake said. "But we don't have time to extract whatever it is from them, and we're not about to resort to torture." He turned back to Defleur. "We obviously need to find a way to leave this system. I'm not sure how we're going to accomplish that yet, but I do know that your cooperation will be a major boon to the effort. Do I have that cooperation?"

Defleur nodded, and the other board members murmured their assent. "The *Javelin* still has a working wormhole generator," Defleur said. "Or at least, it should. It was the only one that was kept disconnected from Ochrim's master control, meaning it was the only one that wasn't damaged irreparably. We haven't generated any wormholes since the one we used to reach this system, but as far as I know, the *Javelin*'s generator does still work."

"Then we have a way out," Jake said, and Lisa was surprised by how much relief he allowed into his voice. He returned his gaze to Lisa, and then to the other members of Oneiri. At last, his gaze drifted to Rug, and to Tessa, who was fiddling with a silver band of some sort. When she flicked it, it snapped into place, becoming stiff, and when she bent it, the band rolled into a circle.

"Lisa Sato," Rug said staring directly at her. "You once promised me that you would help me to reclaim my people's ship, hidden in the Outer Ring. Now that you have the means to keep that promise, do you intend to?"

Lisa hesitated, her gaze on Jake. "I was always going to keep my promise, Rug. But to do it, we'll need at least half of the Darkstream battle group, including one of the destroyers. Even with them, though, I'm not sure how likely we are to succeed out there." *Or to survive.*

"If we can reach my hidden ship, our firepower will increase significantly," Rug said.

Jake blinked. "Hold on. Rug, your ship must have the capacity for interstellar travel, too."

"My ship has a warp drive," the Quatro said. "However, it does not have the ability to extend the effect to other ships."

"Ah. There goes that backup plan, then." His lips pressed together, and as he cast his gaze to Oneiri Team, Rug, and Tessa, his jaw muscles clenched visibly. "We're going to split up the battle group. Lisa and Rug, you'll take half to the Outer Ring, and we'll take the other half."

"To where?" Lisa asked.

"To evacuate as many people from Alex as possible. I refuse to let what happened to Eresos happen there, too. We aren't Darkstream," Jake said while shooting a hard look at Defleur and the others. "We aren't in this strictly for our own self-interest. We're going to save as many innocent people as we can.

And while we're preparing to leave Valhalla, I want it broadcasted to the entire station that anyone who wants to leave is welcome to join us. That includes any soldiers willing to surrender to us. Spirit, I'm putting you on getting that message out."

Marco nodded.

Lisa felt her mouth quirk involuntarily. "Quentin Cooper and his Daybreak goons still hold Habitats 1 and 2. It's probable he's moved on the others, too—system net access was cut off for the entire planet, so it's a reasonable assumption."

"Hopefully he *has* moved on them," Jake said. "That will mean his forces are spread thin." Jake turned to walk toward his alien mech, then he faced the others once more. "I'll put out a call for every spaceworthy ship in the system to join us at Alex, to help with the evacuation. Once we're finished, we'll push out to meet you and Rug in the Outer Ring, Lisa. From there, we're just going to have to pray that the wormhole generator on the *Javelin* is functioning."

"To where will we open the wormhole?" Defleur said, her voice a little deflated from before.

"Well..." Jake said, clearly considering the question. "The way I see it, we're going to have two sizable cohorts representing two species. By now, the use of dark tech is likely completely illegal in the Milky Way, and we have to take that into consideration: if we return there using a wormhole, they probably won't look kindly on it."

"We cannot return to the Quatro Home Systems," Rug said flatly.

Jake tilted his head. "Oh?"

"The Assembly of Elders has established a brutal regime that's wholly intolerant of insubordination. Every Quatro that returned would be put to death for our decision to separate from Quatro society, and I doubt you would be treated much better."

"All right, then," Jake said. "The Milky Way it is."

CHAPTER 35

Last Goodbye

"Lisa, can I speak with you?" Jake called out across the landing bay amidst the bustle of everyone preparing to depart the station.

She nodded. "Sure, Jake."

They exited together into the corridor just outside the landing bay, which was empty.

Jake glanced back into the landing bay just as the hatch was closing behind Lisa. Landing Bay Theta had been the one he'd used the day he first came to Valhalla Station, with Bronson.

That seemed like a million years ago, and looking back at the person he'd been then was like remembering a little kid. He remembered Roach slamming him against the side of the shuttle Bronson had brought him in on. *I'd never tolerate that, now.*

"Will we take the risk of getting out of our mechs to talk?" he asked Lisa.

"Sure. I...I would like to see you."

"Okay." He ordered the alien mech to terminate the dream and release him, which it did. It made him glad that Lisa had said yes to getting out of the mechs. There were still

Darkstream soldiers at large throughout the station, not to mention Roach. But Jake considered this worth it, to snatch a last bit of human interaction before they parted ways, possibly forever.

"What's up?" she said, blinking away sleep as she circled to the front of her mech. Giving her head a shake, she said, "I'm still not used to going to sleep and waking up so many times in one day."

"You'll get used to it," he said. "I brought you out here to talk about Andy. He's insisting—demanding, really—that I let him come with you. But if we really are reforming Oneiri Team, it's important to maintain the chain of command, and right now, I'm at the top of it. Letting him subvert that just because he feels like it doesn't seem like a great precedent."

"Well, are you going to need him on Alex?"

Jake shrugged. "Right now, it's mostly about the principle of the thing. I'm inclined to deny him his demand, for the simple reason that he came to me and demanded it. But the real question is, do you think *you're* going to need him out in the Belt?"

Lisa hesitated. "I'm going to need some backup, but honestly, I'd prefer a more experienced pilot. If you send Andy with me, then we're just a couple of rookies on a mission that already doesn't look great for us."

"What about Beth?"

Slowly, Lisa nodded. "I'd feel better with Arkanian. Despite her recent switch in allegiance."

"Okay," Jake said. "It's settled."

"How are you holding up?" Lisa asked, her head tilting to the side, raven hair swaying.

"I'm...better. For a while, all I could think about was losing Sue Anne, and how dire everything's seemed since she died. But I still have my mom and dad, not to mention plenty of the friends and neighbors we grew up with. I *have* to remember that. I've been so focused on the fact that if something happens to them, I won't be able to live with myself. But just then, in that landing bay, I realized that the only thing *that* means is it's not an option for me to let anything get in the way of us all leaving this system."

"It's true," Lisa said softly. "Though it took me a long time to realize, too. Did you know, when you arranged the meeting between my father and I, I used the opportunity to act like a terrible daughter?"

Slowly, Jake shook his head. "How?"

"He tried to persuade me that our attempt to build a society here in the Steele System has failed. I wouldn't believe him. I thought we could fight to hold onto it. But he was right after all, and now I might never get the chance to tell him. I might never get the chance to say I'm sorry."

"I can have the message passed on, if you like. While we're en route to Alex."

"Would you? I'd truly appreciate it."

"Of course. And Lisa...we're *going* to make it through this. You will speak to your father again. I promise."

"Thank you." Lisa stepped forward, and Jake automatically swept her into an embrace, holding her tightly against him. Her face turned up toward his, and then her lips were pressing against his cheek. "Thank you," she repeated, in a whisper that made Jake's heart beat so hard that he wondered whether Lisa could feel its pulse.

" *Price.*"

The single syllable, spoken in that world-worn voice, turned Jake's stomach to ice. He released Lisa, and he turned to behold his worst fear.

It was Gabriel Roach. Both arms had taken the form of long-barreled cannons already crackling with energy.

Jake was too far from his mech to react in time. If Roach wanted to kill him, his opportunity to do so had come.

CHAPTER 36

Deficient

"Roach," Jake said, refusing to let his fear show in his voice or on his face. "Do your worst to me. Just leave Lisa out of this."

"No," Roach said, raising his weapons, and Jake's throat clenched, as though squeezed by an invisible fist.

"No, you don't understand," Roach went on, and gradually it dawned on Jake: Roach had raised his arms in a gesture meant to be placating. It just so happened that those arms had already taken the form of energy weapons primed to fire, which made the move a lot less comforting.

"Why are you here, Roach?" Jake said.

"I want to help you fight the enemy. The real enemy."

"Out of the question."

"Please," Roach said, and the word sounded odd coming from him. Jake had never known his old commander to use many manners. "Let me finish. I've realized how misguided I've been. I fought the Quatro to get revenge for Jess, but the Quatro were never the real enemy. These shadows, who've sent their metal killers against us—*that's* who we need to defeat."

"You almost killed Ash," Jake said. "You ran her through, and it's basically a miracle she survived. You *did* kill Richaud. There's no way we can trust you, Roach. You spent that coin a long time ago."

Roach was becoming visibly more agitated, and his gun-arms twitched upward once more. Jake had to suppress a wince. "This *thing* made me do that," Roach said. "Except, I've finally learned to control it. Didn't Sweeney tell you? She set me free from Darkstream's containment cell, and I was able to stop myself from killing her or her allies. I targeted Darkstream instead. Give me another chance, Price. I deserve it. I can be valuable to you."

Lie, Jake urged himself. *You need to lie.*

He needed to tell Roach that they *would* welcome him back. He needed to maintain that fiction until he was back inside his own mech, and he could finish Roach off.

But Jake had never had it in him to deal in falsehoods. Even if he could bring himself to try, he doubted the attempt would be very convincing.

Out of nowhere, he remembered an ancient vid he'd come across once while skimming the system net, of a zoologist from Old Earth, studying silverback gorillas in the wild. One of the gorillas had charged at him unexpectedly, but the zoologist hadn't flinched, and his total lack of fear had repelled the animal. Sheer instinct had gripped the gorilla, causing it to turn and scurry away. Because, to it, if the zoologist lacked fear there had to be a reason.

Is Roach so unlike that gorilla? Jake had a good idea of how fragmented the man's mind must be—if it was even correct to call him a man, anymore. The alien mech had the power to dismantle the user's psyche, turning a rational human into something that closely resembled a wild animal, full of primal strength and rage.

"The answer is no," Jake said, his voice steady, commanding. His eyes were riveted to Roach's face, or at least the closest thing he had to a face anymore.

For a long time, Roach returned his gaze, perfectly still—other than his energy-cannon arms, which wavered up and down.

"What about *you?*" Roach hissed at last. "What will become of you once your mech succeeds in taking apart your mind, and you start attacking your allies like I did?"

"That won't happen," Jake said, his eyes riveted to Roach's face.

"Why wouldn't it?"

"Because I still have my humanity. You lost yours long before you ever stepped inside that mech."

The alien mech's head jerked. "You...you're saying I'm...*deficient?*"

"You made yourself deficient. Now, go. Go and accept the fate you know that you deserve."

Roach raised his energy weapons till they were leveled at Jake, and for a long time they stood there, all three of them in fraught tableau.

At last, Roach spun on his heels and charged back down the corridor, away from the landing bay and toward the Core.

CHAPTER 37

State of Play

Commander Stephanie Yates, who was now captain of the *McDougal*, did not seem thrilled by Lisa's and Rug's presence inside the destroyer's CIC.

During the first seven hours of the journey, Lisa had done her best to remain unobtrusive, and to interfere with the ship's operations as little as possible. Her companion did likewise, though of course that was Rug's nature.

As they neared the section of the Outer Ring where Rug said the Quatro ship was hidden, Lisa's silence became less and less viable.

"Captain, if you could have your sensor operator scan nearby planetesimals one more—"

"I've had Jacobs tracking the trajectory of every comet in sight," Yates snapped, "which is taking up significant computer resources, by the way. I've certainly had him continuously scanning for ships. There's nothing here, Seaman Sato."

Lisa didn't like Yates's insistence on making frequent use of her rank, and she liked the woman's tone less. But rebuking her would have signaled insecurity to the CIC crew, and ultimately she and Rug were at their mercy. Lisa needed to project strength and certainty.

They're at our mercy, too, she reminded herself. Neither Rug nor Lisa had left their mechs, and Rug alone wielded sufficient strength to render the destroyer inoperable—a fact of which Yates seemed bitterly aware. Every other UHF ship was in the same situation: each had over a hundred Quatro aboard, more than enough to keep the humans working for Darkstream in line.

"It is almost as though the Meddlers are aware of my hidden ship's existence," Rug subvocalized over an encrypted two-way channel.

"That's not what *I* would have said their absence indicates," Lisa said.

"Consider that their numbers are sufficient to cover most of the Outer Ring. Why this gap in their containment? I sense a trap, with my ship used as bait."

"Are you suggesting we abandon the mission?" Lisa was pretty sure she knew the answer to that, but she had to ask.

"No. I am sorry, Lisa Sato, but though our friendship grants me great trust for you, I cannot say the same for the rest of your species. It is important that the surviving Quatro in this system gain a ship that *we* control. It is much less than we arrived with, but we deserve at least this, especially considering our contributions so far."

Lisa nodded, drawing glances from the captain and her officers, who weren't privy to their conversation. "I'm not disagreeing with that, Rug. I was only asking." She cleared her throat.

"What do you know about the capabilities of the ships Marco spotted out here?" Lisa took the opportunity to tell her implant to call up images of the Meddler ships, which Marco had sent to the resistance leaders, as well as to everyone in Oneiri. The ships were gray, oblong spheroids, unremarkable in almost every way other than their size—twice that of the *Providence*, which was one of the largest ships the UHF ever built.

The quad's eyes glowed brighter as Rug answered. "When they decimated the fleet we brought to this system, they used a mix of conventional weaponry and weapons well beyond my species' capability to produce."

"What do the Quatro consider conventional weaponry?"

"Kinetic weapons. Lasers. Guided missiles."

Lisa nodded, then gestured for Rug to continue, drawing more glances from the CIC crew, whose eyes tracked the movements of the MIMAS' fingers. "All right. What was new to you?"

"The Ravagers themselves serve as the ammunition for one weapon we hadn't encountered before. We believe that is part of why the Meddler vessels are so large—they must have immense manufactories aboard, where they mass produce the Ravagers from raw materials."

"So they...*launch* Ravagers at other ships?"

"Yes. In extremely high numbers, and at extremely high velocities."

"Hmm." She could see how that could be effective. "It only takes a few to get past point defense systems, I guess."

"Yes. Once Ravagers have breached a ship, panic spreads quickly among her crew. Battling them in the corridors is one thing. If the Ravagers breach the hull near critical systems..."

"Right. What else do they have?"

"Particle weapons."

That made Lisa swallow. Humanity's own experiments with particle beams had ended in mostly disappointment, and some tragedy, too. Human engineers had never been able to prevent particle beams from becoming de-focused by ambient electric or magnetic fields—at least, they'd been able to do it over short distances, but not distances meaningful for space combat. They'd also had a lot of trouble making the weapons efficient enough, and the biggest prototype had exploded, destroying the ship it was on, after unexpectedly dumping all its waste heat into it .

But if the Meddlers had made particle beams work, they would have a huge advantage. Particle weapons would be many times more devastating than the lasers wielded by Darkstream's aged warships.

Lisa had fallen silent for a while, and Rug said, "You are concerned by what I've told you."

"Yes."

"You should be."

"Well, we can't let it intimidate us, can we? This is just the state of play, and we can only work with it."

"As you say, Lisa Sato."

CHAPTER 38

Return to Habitat 2

Habitat 2 had no automated defenses, though it did have a lot of heavily armed drug smugglers on its roof, and they all seemed to have itchy trigger fingers.

One of them fired a rocket at Ash as she descended toward Alex. *Screw this.* She ordered her parachute to detach, relying on aerospike thrusters alone to carry her the rest of the way. She handily evaded the next rocket that came at her, and then she returned the love by retracting her mech's fingers against its wrists and opening fire with both rotary autocannons.

The rocket man went down, his pressure suit perforated in dozens of places, while Ash's sky flashed a pleasurable rosy shade.

Her first instinct had been to go for the heavy machine gun on her back, but Jake had ordered them to refrain from firing anything that might compromise the integrity of Habitat 2 and let all the atmosphere out.

Ash felt up to that challenge. If she got the opportunity to bake some coked-out slaver with her flamethrower today, she'd be a pretty happy MIMAS pilot.

She landed on Habitat 2's roof, the metal creaking beneath her, but she hadn't hit hard enough to break anything. A nearby Daybreak slaver had been firing on one of the other descending mechs, but now he turned to confront her.

A bayonet found the throat of his suit, and the reinforced fabric didn't do very much to arrest the force Ash put behind the blade. A red, crystallized mist sprayed from the wound.

Andy Miller landed his MIMAS nearby, and he threw himself at the nearest Daybreak soldier, his rancor partially making up for his lack of skill. Both MIMAS and gunman went down in a heap, and Ash chuckled to herself as she bathed them both in flame.

"Hey!" Andy said, pushing himself to his feet over the blackened form of the dead man. "That hurts!"

"It's just the mech dream simulating pain. You're not actually hurt." *Pansy.*

Jake slammed into Habitat 2's roof a dozen meters away, and Ash felt it tremor from the weight of the alien mech. He pounded away across the rooftop, toward where a handful of defenders were taking cover. Then Maura Odell landed, and she leapt into action immediately, whipping her heavy machine gun from her back to pick off Daybreak fighters.

In less than a minute, they'd cleared the area, just in time for the shuttles full of Quatro to start swooping in and depositing their troops at ground-level.

"The freight elevator can only accommodate one mech at a time," Jake said over the team-wide. "And our Quatro friends aren't getting in through the ground-level airlocks unless we let them in. That means a single mech is going to have to hold the base of that elevator until another can join him."

"Him?" Ash said. "Why are we assuming it's going to be a him?"

"Because *I'm* going down there. The alien mech is the only one I trust to withstand the sort of firepower I expect them to launch at us."

"Typical," Ash said, but she injected enough mirth into her tone to let Jake know she was joking.

He entered the elevator, patching his visual feed through to their HUDs so they could watch what was going on.

The doors opened onto Habitat 2's sterile interior, with its ground-to-roof structures, all lit up by parallelogram lights designed to simulate sunlight.

Looks like he was right about the amount of resistance. Armor-piercing rounds from heavy guns set on tripods, a steady stream of rockets—Quentin Cooper's fighters clearly didn't share Oneiri's concern about breaching the walls of Habitat 2 and letting the oxygen out.

Unsurprisingly, Jake held his own, giving as good as he got and killing half a dozen operatives before the freight elevator returned to the roof again.

Andy stepped toward it, but Ash intercepted, putting a hand against his MIMAS' chest. "I'm next."

"Seriously?"

"You better believe it." She walked inside and maintained eye contact with Miller until the doors blocked him from view.

As the elevator descended, bringing her closer and closer to joining up with Jake, Ash thought about Jess, as she often did whenever she got a rare moment of quiet.

She mostly avoided quiet, and Jess was a major reason why. Ash had never wanted to fully acknowledge the role her sister's memory had played in driving her to become a MIMAS pilot, and then in her mission to kill as many Quatro as possible.

But she'd finally realized what Gabriel Roach could never manage to: honoring Jess's death wasn't about causing even more death. Seeking vengeance only disgraced her memory.

The right way to honor her was to fight as hard as she could to get to a place of peace and stability—for her, for her friends, and for all humans.

Here, today, in the Steele System, that seemed like an impossible dream. But even if she died fighting for it, then she knew Jess would be proud.

Sometimes, she wondered if Jess was watching somewhere, and if she did, how she felt about Ash's actions.

If you're out there, you can stop feeling ashamed of me, sister. You can start feeling proud of me. Because I'm going to make you proud.

The elevator doors opened to Jake's back, which was immediately thrown into sharp relief by a rocket exploding mere meters away from him, detonated by one of his energy blasts.

The bright threads of heavy machine gun fire bracketed him as Ash moved up to join him, scanning for the weapons operators as she raised her rotary autocannons.

There. Instead of high-velocity rounds, she directed lasers at the target, which went up in flames seconds later.

Marco joined them next, and together, they pushed to the nearest vehicle bay, where they let in Quatro by the dozens.

After that, the battle only lasted another forty minutes longer. Habitat 2 was theirs.

"No sign of Quentin Cooper anywhere," Tessa Notaras said in front of the Constable Station, where Jake had called a hasty meeting. "Looks like he's moved on since taking over this place."

Jake nodded. "I'm putting Councilman Pichenko on coordinating the evac from this habitat. He's good with that sort of thing. The rest of us are hitting Habitat 1."

CHAPTER 39

Many

R ug guided the *McDougal*'s Nav officer toward a slightly misshapen, oblong comet, then she asked her to expand the view until the icy mass filled the entire viewscreen.

"The comet's appearance has changed in the twenty years since I last laid eyes on it," Rug said. "But I'm confident this is it."

"That's your ship?" Lisa said, using her MIMAS' amplifiers for the benefit of the CIC crew. "How are we supposed to access it?"

"My quad should get us inside fairly quickly. Originally, we planned to drill through the ice to reach the ship, but that would take time we don't have."

Nodding, Lisa faced Captain Yates. "Captain, we're going to need every combat shuttle from every ship on standby, ready to start transporting Quatro to their ship the moment I say so."

"Understood," Yates ground out.

Lisa and Rug made their way to the destroyer's shuttle bay in silence. They found Beth Arkanian waiting for them near the

airlock, and when she saw them approach, she gave the signal
for the doors to be opened without bothering to greet them.

A couple minutes later, they were outside: two MIMAS
mechs and one quad rocketing toward the great mass of ice.

"There is still no sign of the Meddlers," Rug said in her usual
calm bass.

"They're pretty much everywhere in the Outer Ring but
here," Arkanian said. "Do they really think we're buying that we
got this lucky?"

"I think we're probably acting exactly as they want us to act,"
Lisa said.

"What else can we do?"

"Exactly."

As they neared, Rug began hitting the ice with measured
blasts of energy. Within seconds, a hole opened, and less than a
minute later she'd widened it enough to fly a shuttle through
with room to spare; even the old, clunky UHF combat shuttles
would fit.

Beyond, Lisa could see only blackness—until they passed
through. Then the lights from their suits played across the
ship's hull, and she saw that it was a glimmering purple, like a
Quatro who'd just pulled itself onto a river's bank.

An airlock opened, and Lisa flashed back to getting carried
through underground tunnels on Alex by the invisible force
wielded by the Quatro. Back then, in the darkness of the tunnel,
she hadn't registered the airlock's color, but now she saw it
matched the rest of the hull.

Inside, she immediately saw that here, away from the corrosive effects of a planet's atmosphere, this ship had been better preserved. It lacked the aged look that Rug's subterranean ship had. The swirling colors that covered the walls, deck, and ceiling were more vibrant, and the prevalence of that royal purple was even more striking.

"It will take some time for life support to come on," Rug said. "But I have sent the command."

Back on Alex, the beautiful artwork adorning the interior of the Quatro ship had seemed a bit off, yet comforting. Here, it seemed perfectly appropriate, probably because of how much time Lisa had spent around the thoughtful, gentle Quatro.

They're gentle to their friends, anyway.

There was more than enough room for the trio of mechs to walk side-by-side as they traversed the wide corridors that sloped gently downward, occasionally joining with other corridors, all which seemed to point in the same direction—toward the heart of the vessel.

"How will we get free of the ice encasing the ship?" Lisa asked.

"It should be simple enough," Rug said. "I can have the computer analyze it for weak points, and after that, a few well-placed kinetic kill-masses should cause the shell of ice to shatter."

At last, they came to what had to be the ship's bridge. It took the shape of a sphere, with wide platforms featuring seats that reminded Lisa of the odd furniture she'd encountered on the other Quatro ship. These seats were sleek and metallic, and provisioned with straps that poked up from one side, no doubt used to secure a Quatro in place during battle.

Each "chair" was completely surrounded by a circular console with movable metal parts, and the highest platform bore the largest console. Rug went to that one, and at her approach, a portion of it slid aside to permit her access.

Judging by the temperature readout from Lisa's HUD, life support had succeeded in warming the ship with surprising speed, though not by very much.

That makes sense. Quatro ships would be kept at below freezing, to allow the aliens to manipulate objects as needed. *That must make running water a challenge. They probably have to keep their pipes heated.*

Rug's chair rotated, seemingly unbidden, and she lowered herself onto it, flipping several of the console's bulky metal switches.

Next, the walls themselves came alive with what Lisa recognized as readouts from critical systems, visual feeds, and...

...and a tactical display, which showed them surrounded by over a dozen Meddler ships.

Swarms of Ravagers had already been fired, and were crossing the distances between the enemy and allied ships with alarming speed. The UHF ships' turrets were working overtime, but Lisa was far from certain that they'd be able to hold out much longer.

"It seems kinetic kill-masses will not be necessary to free ourselves from the ice," Rug said, and less than a second later,

Lisa watched as the ice surrounding the Quatro ship shattered with the impact of the first Ravager wave.

"Is there anything we can do about that?" Arkanian asked, her voice strained.

"I have slaved tactical functions to my console and ordered our automatic defenses to neutralize as many Ravagers as possible, but some have already made it to the hull and are burrowing through it as we speak. The enemy struck when we were most vulnerable—the ice made it possible for them to get close to the hull without fear of reprisal."

"How many Ravagers can we expect to have to deal with inside the ship?" Arkanian asked.

Rug paused for a moment, then she answered: "Many."

CHAPTER 40

Detach Parachutes

Habitat 1 sat on a sharp rise, commanding a view of the surrounding terrain for kilometers.

Jake had sent the most talented shuttle pilot from among the five warships to perform a recon flyby, and from that, he'd learned that a ground assault from the bottom of the hill would prove tedious.

Luckily, Jake and the other four mechs accompanying him were dropping in from space instead.

The recon run had also told him that Quentin Cooper was almost certainly inside this habitat. The pilot had spotted twenty-one beetles tricked out with plated armor and swivel-mounted heavy machine guns sitting in strategic spots all around the hillside. There were also over a hundred fighters positioned on the habitat's roof, most of them carrying rocket launchers, though some of them had assault rifles. He spotted a handful of snipers thrown in the mix, too.

Cooper's here, all right. And he knows we're coming.

Jake's mech didn't need the ablative heat shield, parachute, and aerospike thrusters that the MIMAS mechs used for reentry. His biggest challenge involved slowing his descent enough for the others to keep pace.

"Tessa," he subvocalized. "You keeping up?"

"You know I am, boy."

"Stay ready to peel away if the heat's too much. I mean it. If you're in danger of losing shuttles, let us mop up some of the resistance and then come in after us."

"All right. But I'm not letting you hog all the fun."

The other mechs' ablative heat shields had disintegrated several minutes ago, and as Habitat 1 resolved below, becoming a growing silver mass glinting amidst Alex's sapphire landscape, their parachutes deployed.

"Be ready to cut your chutes loose and coast in on aerospike," Jake ordered over the team-wide. "I expect this to get interesting fast."

"You kidding?" Maura Odell said. "This'll be just like Habitat 2. Might have a few more dents in my MIMAS to show for it, that's all. If..."

Odell trailed off as something strange happened with one of the lower hills nearby. The blue surface seemed to peel back, exposing a flat plane underneath lined with white lights.

"What the hell?" Odell said.

"That's a landing strip." No sooner than Marco had spoken he words, a fighter jet burst from the opening in the hillside and flung itself into the air. A second one followed hot on its heels, then a third, and a fourth. Soon, a squadron of eight fighters were in the air, spreading out and heading straight for the five mechs.

"Detach your parachutes!" Jake yelled. "*Detach your para-chutes!*"

CHAPTER 41

The Lie

Lisa charged through the Quatro ship in her MIMAS, following the solid bar of light that Rug had activated for her, which led her up and up along ramped, curving corridors.

She came to a dead end, where the glowing white bar terminated abruptly.

But only for a few seconds. The wall where the light ended rose into the ceiling, and the glowing bar extended for a few meters more.

Lisa dashed forward, and the wall where the dead end had been closed behind her. The one in front of her opened, then, revealing the inky black of space. Out here in the Outer Ring, the stars were the clearest she'd ever seen them. Clearer even than back at Hub.

She threw herself from the ship, twisting as her hands split apart and drew back to rest against her wrists.

There. She fired, picking off a Ravager before it could burrow through the Quatro ship's hull, which Rug had said was called the *Morning Light.* Her HUD highlighted a second Ravager for her, making it glow red in her sights, and when she took that one out it showed her a third.

Using the thrusters built into her arms and calves, Lisa soared past the purple hull, fighting the vertigo that tried to twist her stomach into knots.

She encountered a patch of five Ravagers working together to tear a massive hole in the *Morning Light*.

Whipping the heavy machine gun from her back, Lisa lined up her shot. A short burst across the hull took out three of the Ravagers at once, and the fourth fell just as quickly, but the fifth robot scurried through the hole they'd created and disappeared.

Cursing, Lisa used her calf thrusters to propel her farther along the hull, to deal with the next group.

The heavy machine gun neutralized the Ravagers in less time than her autocannons, and she was able to take out a dozen more in the space of two minutes.

It wasn't nearly enough. All over the hull, Ravagers were disappearing through the holes they'd made. It would be everything Rug and Arkanian could do to prevent them from tearing the vessel apart from the inside. Lisa knew the Ravagers would have the advantage—whereas her allies would have to obey the layout of the ship, the murderous robots could tear through bulkheads at will, making their way toward vital components in a more or less straight line.

She replaced the heavy gun on her back, deciding she could get more work done by targeting two Ravagers at a time with her autocannons.

The first two went down quickly, but as she lined up her next shots, her vision went snowy, and a frenetic hissing noise blocked out all other sound.

Is something wrong with my sensors? She tried firing her autocannons anyway, but she found that she had no control over them.

Gradually, the snow cleared. Instead of the battle outside the Quatro ship, green fields stretched before her, crisscrossed with roads and fences, and dotted with houses and trees and livestock.

As her eyes followed the terrain to the horizon, she blinked, shaking her head. There *was* no horizon. The land curved up and away, and...

...and circled back overhead. Up there, there were also houses and tree and cattle—hanging upside-down.

She was in Hub.

But Hub was exactly like she remembered it. Not overrun by Ravagers. Not overrun by anything.

"Lisa," a warm voice called, and she turned to find Jake, ambling across a field toward her, hands stuck into the pockets of a pair of blue jeans.

"Jake?"

He drew near enough that he had to crane his neck to look at her mech's face. "Hi."

"This is Hub, isn't it? And it's...it's okay. It's just like I remember."

Jake's smile widened. "Oh, yeah. I lied to you about the attack. That never actually happened. Kind of ridiculous to think it would, when you think about it."

"Why would you lie to me about something like that?"

Jake shrugged.

"I don't love you anymore, Jake," Lisa said.

He nodded. "Andy will be relieved to hear that."

CHAPTER 42

Do Not Think

A Ravager tore into the corridor ahead of her, and Rug barreled toward it, up the gentle incline until she was upon the foe.

A swipe of her mechanized paw was all it took to send it flying into the bulkhead, where it shattered.

The ship sent the closest Ravagers' locations to her HUD, which then painted a glowing strip over reality that would lead her along the quickest route to the robots.

Rug galloped along that strip for everything she was worth.

When she'd finally boarded her ship, which she and her people had so carefully hidden in the Outer Ring, it had filled her with blissful relief—only to be cut short by the arrival of the Meddlers.

Had the enemy inferred the ship's existence from the fact that the UHF warships had headed toward it, or had they known about it all along? Neither possibility was comforting, but the latter implied disturbing things about the nature of the Meddlers' interactions with humanity and the Quatro.

The Meddlers have already taken everything from my people once. I will not allow them to take my ship!

She reached the next group of Ravagers just as they were burrowing through an inner bulkhead. Two of them fell to energy blasts, but a third squeezed through the rent it had created before Rug could take care of it.

No!

Burrowing through that bulkhead would take it near one of her ship's primary engines. That could not come to pass.

Rug turned and ran back the way she'd come, headed for a corridor closer to the engine, in the hopes of intercepting the metal beast. Her quad's speed was such that her momentum nearly took her past the required turn, and her left side slammed into the bulkhead as she veered, leaving a shallow dent.

Nothing compared to what the Ravagers are doing to my vessel.

"Beth Arkanian," Rug subvocalized as she ran. "How are you faring on the starboard side?"

"As well as can be expected," Arkanian answered, her voice strained. "I think the rate of infiltrations has slowed—the ship's arsenal must finally be having an effect, now that the ice isn't blocking it. But, Rug...I think there are too many of them already inside."

"Do not *think*," Rug said as she caught up with the Ravager who'd been headed toward the engine. She blasted it to bits. "Only help me save my ship."

They both fell silent as they waged their separate battles against the endless metal marauders. The ship began directing

Rug to the Ravagers who were closest to vital systems, and whose trajectories were likely to take them there. It seemed that each Ravager she destroyed had made it closer to a critical ship component than any before it.

Soon, they will dismantle her. And I doubt we'll have time to effect the necessary repairs.

She rounded a corner to behold five Quatro battling with an equal group of Ravagers. One of the robots tore a wicked gash in the side of the Quatro closest to Rug, and Rug overcame her shock in order to take the bot apart with high-velocity rounds.

"Brothers and sisters!" she yelled. "I did not think the humans would manage to get a shuttle through the onslaught they're suffering."

"Three shuttles have made it through," the wounded Quatro answered. "Two more have docked on the other side of the *Morning Light.*"

"Then perhaps there is hope for her."

A transmission came through, then—from Stephanie Yates, captain of the *McDougal.* Her likeness appeared in the corridor beside Rug.

"I have some bad news for you, uh, Rug," the captain said, seeming to stumble a little on the name Rug had chosen for herself in order to interact properly with humans.

Somehow, Rug knew what Yates was about to tell her, even thought she'd yet given no indication of it.

Even so, she asked: "What is it?"

"Your friend, Sato...her mech went strangely immobile, and we could do nothing to get in contact with her. A group of Ravagers descended on her."

"Has Lisa Sato been killed, Stephanie Yates?"

"I don't know. But she seemed alive when we saw her last. The Ravagers didn't kill her—they engaged thrusters and took her inside one of the enemy ships."

CHAPTER 43

High-Risk

The squadron of fighters sent kinetic impactors screaming into all five mechs, though the MIMAS didn't weather the storm nearly as well as Jake's alien mech did.

I need to do something. As he slowed his descent with streams of fire projecting from his calves, he turned his arms into energy cannons that he swept across the aircraft, fragmenting their formation and causing five of the eight jets to peel away.

Three continued on, though, and now Jake was their primary target. They each sent two missiles at him of unknown make, following up with guns.

The fighters started to launch another missile salvo, but Jake was ready for it, having ignored the initial one. He directed his steady stream of energy bolts along a downward diagonal, intersecting with the rightmost jet and exploding one of its missiles as it left the tube. The jet flew straight into the explosion, shearing off one of its wings.

Jake rocketed downward sharply, narrowly evading the first volley of missiles. The five jets that had peeled off were coming around for a pass at the MIMAS mechs, who they'd probably figured out were easier prey.

"They don't look like any jets I've seen," Marco said. "At least, not any meant for combat inside planetary atmospheres."

But in this area, at least, Jake's knowledge exceeded Marco's. He'd always been fascinated by the history of jet and space fighters, and he knew almost every model that had ever been constructed, all the way back to the Me 262.

To Jake, these fighters looked like F-22 Raptors, but with longer wings and a much more spherical body.

"I think those wings retract," he mumbled as the wind whipped past him on his way to Alex's surface.

"Why would they be designed that way?" Marco asked, and Jake blinked. He hadn't realized that he'd broadcasted his muttering.

Clearing his throat, he said, "To allow them to compete in space." Clearly, Cooper wasn't content with dominating only Alex. These space fighters meant he had designs on the entire system, and with Darkstream in decline, that made a lot of sense.

"Target those things with your rockets and be ready to use autocannons to take apart any missiles they send back at you," Jake said.

They were closing with Habitat 1's roof, but that brought its own host of challenges. Suddenly, they were within rocket range, and missiles started streaming up from below as well.

He shook his head to clear it, and then he started speaking rapidly, in order to deliver his next orders fast enough to allow time for their execution:

"Change of plans," he spat. "I want the four of you to aim for spots on the hill where you'll have plenty of cover. You'll need to play a stealthy game in order to take out all those armored beetles without getting taken out yourselves."

"What will you be doing?" Ash asked.

"Taking the roof."

"All by yourself?"

He took a deep breath. "The alien mech is the only one versatile enough to have a chance. They'll have twenty clear firing lanes at anything that lands there. I'm calling off the shuttles until we can deal with this mess—there's no way anything's getting through, as-is."

"Okay. Good luck, Clutch."

"Good luck, Steam. Spirit. Uh...we don't have nicknames for Odell or Miller yet."

"Moe for Odell and Hotshot for Miller," Ash said hastily.

Jake hesitated. "Yeah? Just like that?"

"We tend to lose pilots who don't have nicknames."

With that, Jake landed on the roof. He was in the thick of things, and unable to concentrate on anything except survival.

Dozens of assault rifles came alive, peppering him with rounds, but that was the least of his worries. A rocket streamed at him from point-blank range, directly behind him, and then everything happened at once.

The mech dream saw to it that he reacted appropriately on an emotional level—with a stab of panic underscored by the familiar piercing violin note. A piece of him shot from his lower back, detonating the rocket before it traveled more than a few meters and killing the diminutive man who'd fired it.

After that, an area opened up around Jake with a rapidly widening radius, as his enemies quickly learned to give him his distance. Rockets began streaming toward him from every direction, and he had no time to incorporate conscious thought into his reaction.

The input from the visual sensors covering his body fused with the mech dream's ability to induce instant emotional responses to physical phenomena.

Jake embraced his fear, which screamed at him to favor flight over fight. He twisted left and a rocket sailed underneath his left armpit, while another impacted his right—at least, it would have, if he hadn't commanded the mech to be elsewhere, bunching into itself, compressing, curling around the rocket's trajectory so that there was only empty space where it would otherwise have hit him.

Tiny energy rifles projected from various spots on his body, single-use in the sense that they formed solely to shoot down a rocket and then retract inside him once more.

A sniper rifle round connected with the back of his head, causing it to crack forward and inducing an immediate migraine.

He couldn't afford to take notice of it. Instead, he kept evading missiles; kept ducking and dodging and returning fire at his aggressors whenever he found space to do so.

Five of the seven remaining fighter jets began to fly toward the roof of Habitat 1 for a strafing run, and something inside Jake snapped. He launched himself from the rooftop with a powerful leap, engaging his rockets while firing backward with energy cannons, using his rear sensors to pick off more rooftop targets.

The lead jet sped up, but it couldn't escape him. Jake *widened*, long, sinewy arms lengthening to wrap around the jet in a powerful embrace. The frame buckled inward slightly, and Jake engaged his thrusters at full power, at an angle that forced the jet to flip around and spiral toward the ground.

Originally he'd intended to carry the jet back to the rooftop, to use it as a sort of bomb against those who'd tormented him with their bullets and missiles. The whispers rose up in harmony to encourage the idea.

But doing so would almost certainly cause irreparable damage to Habitat 1, sending its atmosphere whooshing out.

Instead, Jake guided the jet toward the beetle that was farthest from the habitat. He flung the craft toward it, hard enough that there was little the pilot could do to correct its course.

Jet and beetle collided in a spectacular explosion, orange and yellow flames licking the air before Alex's lack of atmosphere quenched them. Jake rocketed back toward the rooftop.

On his way, he took out a dozen or so soldiers wielding rocket launchers, and that was enough to break the spirit of Quentin Cooper's criminals. Having seen what the alien mech was capable of, they fled—some of them toward one of the habitat's two freight elevators, others toward the edge of the roof, where they leapt over the side, likely to suffer injuries and suit breaches when they landed.

"The roof's clear," Jake said over the team-wide, more to boost morale than anything else. He ran to the edge of the roof, directing bolts of crackling energy at beetle after beetle while sparing some for the jets overhead. The other Oneiri pilots had succeeded in taking out almost half of the beetles, and with Jake unleashing superior firepower from an elevated position, they made short work of the rest.

Only four jets remained, now—the MIMAS mechs had succeeded in taking out two more while Jake fought on the roof—and the jet pilots seemed to glean the likely outcome of this battle. They abruptly angled themselves upward and began the steady climb toward space, as they were designed to do.

"All right, then," Jake said. "Good work, Oneiri."

His implant pinged him with a transmission request, and when he approved it, a voice with a British accent came through. "Jake Price, isn't it?"

For some reason, the mech dream didn't simulate a likeness of Cooper—the transmission was audio only. Maye the man had altered his implant to block the function, somehow. "It is. I assume this is Cooper?"

"I have you at no disadvantage, I see."

"Yeah," Jake said. "That seems pretty clear."

"I was referring to knowing your name already."

"I wasn't."

Cooper sniffed. "All right, then. I see we can move straight past the pleasantries. I have a proposition for you, Mr. Price."

"What is it?"

"Leave. Immediately. Let these people continue their lives in peace."

"Do you mean the residents of Habitat 1? You've made them your slaves."

"Yes, but it's better to be a slave than dead, isn't it?"

"What are you talking about?"

"I'm talking about my intention of venting all their oxygen until they suffocate, unless you leave *right now.* If you continue your attempts to infiltrate this habitat, there will be no one left for you to save. Be a good boy and leave us be."

"There are emergency protocols that will prevent you from doing that. They'll grant us enough time to get the population out."

"Tens of thousands of people live here, Mr. Price. Besides, don't you think I would've already overridden those protocols? It isn't hard to do. I've had control of this place for months, and I've prepared for every eventuality."

Jake fought to slow his breathing. "I don't think you understand, Cooper. We're not leaving without those people."

"And I'm not letting you leave with them alive. You're not very good at this, are you, Mr. Price?"

"Good at what?"

Cooper gave a theatrical sigh. "About now is when, typically, you'd offer me something I want in exchange for my cooperation."

"Okay. What do you want?"

"I want a way to leave this system. I've seen what's happening. I have the sensor data showing thousands of ships waiting to swoop through the system, in all probability leveling everything in their path."

For a long moment, Jake weighed the possibility. "Fine," he ground out at last. "I can grant you safe passage out of the solar system, provided we can secure it for ourselves."

"I don't mean aboard one of your ships. I mean that I *want* a ship. A warship. I want you to allow me to accompany you to wherever you create a wormhole using Bronson's *Javelin*—I know his is the only wormhole generator that still functions. And I also want one of your mechs."

Jake squeezed his eyes shut. He couldn't honor any of Cooper's demands. *Can I?*

"Let's meet face-to-face," Jake said. "This isn't something to be discussed over comlink."

"I won't meet with you, Mr. Price," Cooper said, his tone admonishing. "No, no. You're far too hotheaded. Send in someone with a more even temperament, so that we might discuss matters sensibly. Preferably someone practiced in negotiations. And just *one* individual, Mr. Price. Unarmed. I don't trust you with anything beyond that."

"All right. Where should I send them?"

"The central module you see atop the habitat's roof is an armored observation unit. It's also Habitat 1's master control center, and I've adopted it as my command center. You can send your emissary there."

With that, Cooper terminated the transmission.

Jake's heart was beating so hard it made his vision vibrate—or maybe that was just the mech dream. Either way, he couldn't let the anger he'd let Cooper induce get the better of him.

I'm glad we didn't meet in any other context. That's not a guy I could live with for any length of time.

"Tessa," he said over a two-way channel. "I have an extremely high-risk mission for you, but only if you accept."

"What's the objective?" she said, without hesitation.

"Saving the people of Habitat 1."

"I'm in."

CHAPTER 44

Redemption

The inner airlock door hissed as the seal broke and it lowered into the ground to admit Tessa into Quentin Cooper's command center.

Cooper's jaw dropped the moment she removed her helmet, though she'd been around long enough to recognize a man who saw his every action as part of a performance.

"Tessa *Notaras*," he said, his accent ratcheting a few socioeconomic levels higher than his normal manner of speech. "You know, the possibility that it might be you crossed my mind when I saw you exit the shuttle out on the roof. But I couldn't be sure until your helmet was off. It *is* you."

"It is." Her eyes flitted to the control panel behind him, then back to Cooper's face.

"How *have* you been?" he asked. "We'll need to search you, of course." Cooper snapped his fingers at a pair of guards flanking the airlock, who took it upon themselves to start dismantling Tessa's pressure suit to give her a patdown. One of them even ran his fingers through her white hair, which was held together with a silver band. *So close.*

"How have I been, you ask," Tessa said, her tone musing, as though she wasn't having her personal space invaded by a couple of amoral gorillas. "Do you mean since you murdered most of my Three Points associates?"

An offended expression replaced Cooper's warmth—or at least, an expression meant to simulate offense. "Now, Tessa, I know you didn't take that personally. Tell me you didn't. That was strictly business. Either Daybreak was going to take over this planet or Three Points was—we both know that. I was just the one to move first."

"Neither of us needed to take it over. We had a good thing going, Cooper. A marketplace, and one Darkstream didn't have its fingers in. Until you let them stick their whole hand in, of course."

"Tessa, you can tell me that Three Points didn't spend a considerable amount of time preparing to eventually take over, but I won't believe you. At any rate, to be fair, *my* takeover did work out rather well for me, wouldn't you say?"

"For a few months. Until now. You just lost two habitats."

"But I'm gaining a warship, along with a MIMAS mechs. Not a bad trade for a two-bit drug lord, wouldn't you say?"

"I'm afraid the MIMAS is out of the question. Are we going to stand here staring at each other, or do you have an actual negotiating table?"

"I do, in fact. It isn't much, but it'll do." Cooper waved at a round steel table with two seats, and Tessa walked toward it. "Now, I do find it odd that your starting position appears to be that I can't have a MIMAS mech. That seems to suggest that

you *will* get around to offering me it, eventually, if I know anything about negotiating. But I thought you'd be cannier than—"

Tessa changed directions just before arriving at the table,
sidestepping around Cooper's back and snaking an arm around
his forehead. Simultaneously, she jerked on the end of the silver
band holding her hair together, and the band snapped into her
grasp, rigid, becoming a blade as long as her hand. Her long,
snowy hair cascaded down her back as she pressed the blade to
Cooper's throat.

"Oh, I like my negotiating position quite a lot, actually,"
Tessa said. She began to drag Cooper backward, toward the
control panel.

"She's botched it," the drug lord said, sounding almost resigned. "Shoot her!"

He tried to jerk away, but Tessa's grip was stronger than
he'd anticipated, apparently. He remained in place, but his
goons followed his orders, pumping lead into Cooper as well as
Tessa.

There were at least three bullets inside her by the time she
made it to the control panel, using Cooper as a shield against
the onslaught. The man was likely dead, by now—he'd taken a
lot more abuse than she had.

But Cooper had been right. The memory didn't fill her with
pride, but Three Points *had* spent a lot of time preparing for a
takeover, and she knew a fair bit about a habitat's control systems.

Enough, anyway, to know what to press to let Jake and the
others inside this control center.

She input the command while holding Cooper's corpse close, like a lover.

He absorbed several of the bullets intended for her, but not enough of them. She took more hits, and her breathing was coming in ragged, burbling gasps, now. Her legs gave out underneath her, and she fell backward against the panel, still holding Cooper's body across most of her torso.

As the inner airlock opened to admit Jake inside his alien mech, Tessa thought of Gabriel Roach, oddly.

It occurred to her how similar she and Roach were. Both of them had done horrible things, and both had been completely unable to reconcile those things with the fact that they viewed themselves as fundamentally good people.

Despite that, they'd continued to do the horrible things. They'd continued exposing themselves to that moral abyss.

It hadn't been the alien mech that had disintegrated Roach's psyche. The mech had sped up the process, but that would've always been the end game. He was completely unable to accept either the reality that he'd done evil things or the fact that, for his sanity, he needed to turn around and start doing good.

As her consciousness faded, Tessa knew that she'd also come close to fragmenting.

I didn't quite get there, though. And maybe we can call today a redemption.

Jake made short work of the Daybreak soldiers inside the control center, and then he slid out of his great metal hulk of a mech to kneel at Tessa's side.

"Hang in there," he told her. "We're going to get you back inside a shuttle. Get you to the nicest sick bay those warships have to offer."

Tessa shook her head.

"Come on, Tessa. We have to move, and I need your cooperation for that. I need you to stay with me, okay? We don't have much time. The Meddler ships have started to tighten the noose, with Alex at the center. Soon enough, they'll close around us. If we're going to get out of this system, now is the time."

Tessa shook her head once more. "I'm gone," she managed to croak. "Don't waste any more time on me."

With that, the darkness took her.

CHAPTER 45

Intelligence

Lisa woke to a softly lit room with beige walls and sumptuous leather furniture. Sitting up, she found herself in the embrace of an armchair with just the right amount of stuffing. Before her sat a coffee table carved from mahogany, and while it was clearly expensive, it was understated, too—small, with only a few flourishes included by the craftsperson.

The light level seemed to increase as her eyes adjusted to it, so that they never felt strained by it. Across from Lisa was a long, leather couch the same color as her armchair.

Squeezing her eyes shut, she tried to recall how, or why, she was here. A soft hiss reached her ears, and she opened her eyes once more to find that a rectangular aperture had opened in one of the walls to reveal a tall, thin robot covered in interwoven plates of silver and gold.

Crying out, she leapt to her feet, hand flying to her hip, where she kept her sidearm holstered.

It wasn't there.

The robot made no move toward her—it simply stood there, regarding her, as though waiting for her to piece everything together.

I was outside the Morning Light. *Fighting the Ravagers.*

On the heels of that memory came the realization that this robot matched Rug's description of the ones she'd thought had been under direct control by someone or something. The ones the other robots had done everything they could to protect.

"You...you're a Meddler," Lisa said.

"Very good," the robot answered, moving smoothly to the couch and taking a seat. "Though we prefer to be called Progenitors." It was odd to see a robot in repose, and odder still when it gestured at the armchair Lisa had woken in. "Please. Sit." The aperture closed silently—ominously, especially since it had no visible mechanism for opening it again.

Lisa remained standing.

"There's absolutely nothing you can do to effect an escape from this room until we've had our chat," the Progenitor said. "You can try harming this telepresence robot, but even if you succeeded, it wouldn't have a meaningful effect on...well, on anything."

"Telepresence robot. So that isn't what you actually look like."

"Far from it."

"Why won't you meet with me yourself, then? Are you so cowardly?"

"A number of reasons, a principal one being that you aren't ready to behold our faces. The experience would break you."

"I highly doubt that."

"You'd be surprised. At any rate, it's out of the question. This is the way we will have our discussion."

Lisa decided that accepting the thing's invitation to sit would be the best of her limited options for projecting strength. She suspected that attacking the robot would prove just as futile as it claimed. So she sat.

"You said you prefer 'Progenitor.'" She felt her mouth curl involuntarily, in distaste. "So you view yourselves as...parents, of some sort?" The idea perplexed her, but that *was* the meaning of the word, as far as she could remember it.

"Of a sort, yes," the robot said, nodding, its elongated head turning the motion into a vaguely threatening one. "The word can also mean 'that which originates,' and we have served as the origin of many things. We're only getting started in that regard, in fact."

"What have you...originated?"

"The Gatherers, for one. The Amblers. The Ravagers. The alien mech that your friend Jake Price pilots. And..." The robot held up a spindly hand, palm-up, in a nonchalant gesture. "And the Ixa."

Lisa shook her head. "You're lying. The Ixa weren't *created* by anything. Their evolutionary past is well-studied, well-documented."

"You're right. But we initiated that evolutionary past, Lisa. There's a lot for you to get up to speed on, you know—things that the rest of your species has known for twenty years, now."

"The rest of my species...they're alive?"

"Yes. They won the war. Congratulations, by the way."

Despite herself, a tiny flame of hope flickered inside Lisa. *So there's something for us to return to after all.*

"It was, effectively, a war against us, since the Ixa were our unwitting war hounds. But actually, the term 'battle' might be more appropriate for that conflict—maybe even 'skirmish.' Because the war is far from over, Lisa. Far, far from it. You might say that our little scrimmage here in the Steele System was another battle in the same war; a battle it seems we have won."

"That's wrong," Lisa snapped. "We're not done fighting yet."

"We've won," the Progenitor said, sounding slightly uncomfortable, as though it felt awkward about having to explain this to Lisa. "But that's not what's important. What's important is what all this means for our continuing efforts to exterminate humanity." The thing's voice had gotten increasingly cheerful, putting Lisa in mind of a vid advertisement for some new system net service. "Are you ready to learn?"

She said nothing, not enjoying the sense that she was being toyed with.

"I'm going to assume you are," the Progenitor said. "Okay, so here it comes: everything that's happened here in this system, it was just one big intelligence gathering exercise. How's that for a mind-bender?"

"I can't even begin to unpack that gibberish," Lisa spat.

"My," the robot said, sounding genuinely surprised. "Testy. Okay. Let me help to break it down for you. We engineered Darkstream's arrival in this solar system. For a while now, we've had the ability to tamper with wormholes as they're being created, and we tweaked the one Darkstream used to leave the Milky Way so that it brought you to this specific part of this galaxy. Once your former employer arrived, their exoplanet experts saw that this system was the only one around that showed no signs of colonization. So they selected it and hoped for the best. That was also by our design. Are you with me so far?"

Lisa didn't answer.

"I think you are with me. You're sharp, Lisa, that's well known to us. So, okay. Darkstream chose this system to colonize, and of course they were delighted to find resource exploitation infrastructure already in place—infrastructure far more efficient than anything humanity has had access to before. The only obstacle to using it, of course, were those pesky four-legged giants. The Quatro. But they seemed primitive enough, and humans have always been easy to manipulate when it comes to making them fear and hate something. So Darkstream taught their fighting men and women to hate, and to kill, the Quatro, and all was well with the world.

"Until, that is, Bronson and the Darkstream board of directors learned that the Gatherers' owners were well aware of how they'd hijacked them. We're getting into new territory for you now, aren't we? You see, we approached Bronson and the board soon after that first year—soon after they succeeded in suppressing the Quatro and seizing a healthy share of the resources for themselves. And we cut them a deal. We told them that they were welcome to continue using those resources. We didn't even want a percentage. But we did have one condition."

The Progenitor paused, clearly leaving space for Lisa to say something. She didn't want to play its game, but she did want to know what Darkstream had given them in return. "What was it, damn you?"

"In exchange for the use of our resource-gathering robots, we required Darkstream to build a surveillance apparatus the likes of which humanity has never known. It's perfect, for its purpose—the technology is ours, so of course it's perfect. Since almost the beginning of humanity's little experiment in the Steele System, we've had access to virtually everything that every human here has said or done. Everything in the Steele System was either constructed by Darkstream or using their materials. Everything from the habitats you've lived in to the devices you've used to communicate. We could never have done this without the company's help, but we *did* do it. Through lucid, we practically came to learn some of your thoughts, though of course most of those did escape us. Pity."

"Why did you want to spy on everyone?" Lisa said.

"I'm sorry, didn't I mention already? This was an intelligence gathering exercise, and we have everything we need, which is why the whole thing is coming to such a violent end."

"Intelligence on *what?*"

"Isn't it obvious? On humanity, and on the Quatro. We pitted you against each other, in a war fought solely for our benefit. You see, Lisa, we are very methodical. We've unleashed a super-intelligent AI on every galaxy of the local cluster. Each AI is configured differently, with its own unique set of skills and strategies. It's all part of a grand process of algorithmic evolution, designed to solve the problem of conquering this entire universe. The galaxy we're currently in is one where the AI succeeded with flying colors, and so we will be using it again in the next generation of AIs, to be unleashed on the next cluster of galaxies. We own this particular galaxy now, which is why it was relatively straightforward for us to set up this little experiment involving you and the Quatro. In fact, we've either conquered or are very close to conquering every galaxy in this entire cluster— all except two. The only two galaxies where we were repelled are the Milky Way, where humans are dominant, and Canis Major, where the Quatro are dominant. No doubt you can see why we were so keen to learn about you—about your technology, your weapons, your tactics, your psychology...and, of course, your weaknesses. And we *have* learned, Lisa. We've learned so much. I don't think it's an exaggeration to say that we now have everything we need to exterminate your species."

Lisa felt light-headed as she sat in stunned silence. She could feel how wide her eyes were as she stared at the robot's inhuman face.

"You're very sharp, Lisa, so no doubt you're now wondering why your species has posed such a challenge for us, and why the Quatro have as well. Other than their strength, the Quatro reproduce rather rapidly, which allowed them to overcome even the numbers marshaled by the AI we sent to their galaxy. It also helped that their Assembly of Elders maintains such strict control of the population that they function almost as though they are a single entity. As for why humanity has proven so troublesome, I'll let you in on something that the rest of your species knows, but which you in the Steele System do not. You're familiar with the Kaithe?"

She bobbed her head, still feeling dumbstruck. The Kaithe were a reclusive, childlike species with only one known planet, located along a string of darkgate-connected systems called Pirate's Path.

"Yes, well it turns out the Kaithe created humanity to be a weapon species, just as our AI created the Ixa. Humans were meant to be the Kaithe's very own hounds of war, if you will. Of course, they never ended up using you, and having felt terrible for creating such a warlike species, they turned inward on themselves. We don't have those hangups, obviously."

The corner of Lisa's right eye twitched.

"Oh, dear. I fear I've gone too far—it's all so much for you to take in, isn't it?"

"Why did you tell me *any* of this?" Drawing a deep breath to rally herself, Lisa continued: "My friends will come for me. They won't stop until they find me. And when they do, they'll learn everything you just told me."

The Progenitor nodded. "That's not a problem. In fact, we intend to send you back to them ourselves."

"You...you do?"

The Progenitor's oblong head tilted to one side. "Well...in a sense."

CHAPTER 46

A Selfish Impulse

The arrival of Rug's brethren had spelled an end to the Ravager incursion, and now the Quatro patrolled the corridors of the *Morning Light* while Rug remained on the bridge to coordinate the defense, and also to provide aid to the human warships.

At first, it had been all they could do to keep the Ravagers from tearing the ships apart stem from stern. Now, several hours into the battle, the tide was turning, and if that continued, they should be able to start devoting some of their arsenal to firing back at the Meddler ships.

Except, Rug was reluctant to do so—at least, not at the ship Captain Stephanie Yates had identified as the one to which the Ravagers had taken Lisa Sato.

After Rug had lost her mate, she'd undergone a period of recklessness, during which she'd thrown herself into danger with little concern for her own safety. The whispers that periodically rose up inside the quad encouraged her to continue down that path, and she almost had, even though she'd know oblivion waited at its end.

But then, on the space elevator, remembering what a dear friend she had in Lisa Sato had finally brought her back to her senses, and she'd realized that she did have something to live for. Now that Lisa was taken, Rug scrutinized the tactical display, her entire being focused on finding a way to extract victory from an engagement that showed every sign of ending in defeat.

The Meddlers had not brought their particle beams to bear at all, which she found strange. They'd focused almost exclusively on Ravagers.

Why?

A transmission request came directly to her suit, and she patched it through to one of the wall displays.

It was Jake Price, and despite her command, the mech dream stubbornly rendered him as standing right next to her.

"So this is the inside of a Quatro ship," he said, looking around.

She ordered the wall showing the tactical display to expand its view, and when she did, she saw the massive fleet of ships— mostly civilian—which had just reached the periphery of the engagement.

"You succeeded?" she asked in disbelief. "You evacuated all of Alex?"

"Half of it," he said with reluctance. "The rest of the Meddler ships began sweeping through the system, centering on Alex and attacking everything they encountered along the way. We ran out of time, Rug. We...had to abandon Habitats 3 and 4."

Jake's shoulders fell as he delivered the news. But he still met her eyes. "We lost Tessa Notaras, Rug."

Rug moaned, long and low. It was some time before she found her voice again. "This has rent my soul in two, Jake Price."

"I know. I'm sorry, Rug. But we need to leave this system, now. If these Meddler ships don't take us out, then the others will."

"We...we cannot leave yet, Jake Price."

"What? Why not?"

Rug lowered her head. What she was suggesting went against everything she stood for—against the Quatro way. It was not meant to serve her drift. Instead, it was a selfish impulse, born solely of a desire to save her personal friend.

But she did not care.

"The Meddlers have Lisa Sato," she said slowly. "I will not take my ship away from this place until I have her back."

"We have Lisa."

Rug's head whipped up toward him. "*What?*"

"We picked her up on the edge of the battle, the moment we arrived. She was in her MIMAS—the mech wasn't operational, but Lisa's fine. I'm heading down to the shuttle bay to speak with her the moment we finish our conversation."

Rug breathed a sigh of relief. "Then let us leave this place, Jake Price. Let us leave and never return."

CHAPTER 47

Painful to Watch

Jake started jogging toward the *Melvin*'s shuttle bay even as he terminated the conversation with Rug. As he ran, he sent Bronson a transmission request, and after several long seconds it was accepted.

"Price. What can I do for you?"

"I need you to open the wormhole, now."

"Right. Uh, about that." Bronson rubbed the back of his head. "We actually tried to open it, and we're having trouble with our generator."

"I'm out of patience for you."

"What are you saying?"

"What do you think I'm saying, Bronson? You ordered me to abandon my family to their deaths, and my disobeying that order is the only reason my parents are still alive. I'm saying that my tolerance for your bullshit has bottomed out, and if that wormhole isn't open within fifteen minutes, I'm going to kill you." With that, Jake cut off the transmission and ran faster.

Andy arrived at the hatch leading to the shuttle bay at the same time Jake did, and they studied each other for a few moments. Then Andy hit the control for the hatch and entered without a word.

Jake spotted Lisa standing at the base of her MIMAS, surrounded by the other Oneiri pilots who'd accompanied Jake to Alex. Nearby, the empty mech they'd acquired on Valhalla stood, motionless. After a few seconds, Lisa noticed Jake and Andy, and she jogged across the shuttle bay toward them.

When she reached Jake...she ran straight past him, into Andy's arms, who was nearly knocked off his crutches.

Lisa gave Andy a passionate kiss, which lasted an uncomfortably long time. For reasons Jake wasn't entirely clear on, it was an incredibly painful thing for him to watch, and yet he wasn't able to pry his eyes away from it.

Finally, they came up for air, and a silence stretched on as Andy watched Lisa's face, looking a bit baffled.

"I escaped," she said at last, her gaze shifting from Andy to Jake. "The Meddlers—they call themselves the Progenitors—they captured me, and they managed to get me out of my mech. But I was able to fight my way back to it. They'd done something to the MIMAS, though, and it froze up again shortly after I escaped their ship."

Jake nodded slowly. "Did they say anything to you?"

Lisa's grin broadened. "Did they ever."

Hesitating, Jake asked, "What did they tell you?"

"We beat the Ixa, Jake. Humanity is alive and well in the Milky Way." Her grin faltered a little. "That's the good news, anyway."

"And the bad?"

"The Progenitors are planning to move against the Milky Way with everything they have. The one I spoke to claimed that they created the Ixa."

Jake shook his head. "That would make them pretty damn old. Anything else?"

"No, nothing. I was lucky to get that, don't you think?"

"Yeah," he said slowly. "You were."

"How did things go on Alex?"

"We were able to evacuate half the planet. The other half..." Jake pursed his lips. "That isn't all. Tessa, she...Tessa didn't make it, Lisa."

Lisa's eyes went blank and distant. "God..."

"I'm sorry. Are you, uh, all right?"

"Yeah. Sorry, I'm just going to need a bit to process that. It's a lot."

"Yeah." Jake gestured at the hatch leading to the rest of the destroyer. "I'm going to contact Bronson about opening that wormhole. Let me know if there's anything I can do...okay?"

"Definitely. Thanks, Jake."

"No problem."

As he walked toward the hatch, he glanced back over his shoulder to see Lisa gazing lovingly up at Andy.

Strange...

He wasn't reflecting on the fact she was apparently head-over-heels for Andy, though that was a bit weird. What seemed truly strange to Jake was how little Tessa's death had seemed to affect Lisa.

They were extremely close. And she's acting like Tessa's already forgotten.

Giving his head a shake to clear it, Jake left the shuttle bay.

CHAPTER 48

Just as He Always Did

Bronson trudged through the corridors of the *Javelin* toward his office, for his first meeting with the Progenitor since before Valhalla fell.

He'd been toying with some choice words he planned to use with the thing, but now that the time had come, he wasn't sure it was a good idea. True, the Progenitors had grossly violated their agreement with Darkstream. But they could also very well be his last lifeline. Returning to the Milky Way did not spell very good things for him. A lengthy jail sentence might be the best he could hope for.

He'd lied to Price about the wormhole generator not functioning. As far as he knew, it was working just fine. But he'd needed to buy some time to consult with the treacherous alien robot that lived in a secret closet inside his office.

Once he got there, he used his implant to open the hidden panel that concealed the tall machine. For the first time ever, it was already activated, waiting for him, and it stepped out as soon as Bronson opened up its enclosure.

That made Bronson yell out involuntarily, and he found the edge of his desk with a shaking hand.

"Calm yourself," the robot said. "Sit." It pointed at Bronson's desk chair.

"Why should I?" Bronson said, hating how pathetic he sounded. "You promised us profit, and expansion that never ended. We surveilled our entire population for you!"

"The populace were the ones who sacrificed their privacy unknowingly. You didn't sacrifice anything."

"We had a deal."

"We still have one," the robot said, towering over Bronson's, its gold and silver plates glimmering under the halogens.

"How do you figure that?"

"I need you to have some faith. And to stay silent for a moment so that I can speak. I trust you're capable of that?"

Bronson waited.

"Sit down."

He circled the desk and lowered himself into his chair.

"The data we've compiled on humanity isn't limited to what you've supplied to us," the Progenitor said. "We've also monitored the humans in the Milky Way, though not nearly with the granularity of detail we had access to here, of course. Using what we've learned, we're confident that we can bring about Darkstream's resurgence in your old galaxy. You can come to dominate your society again—but this time, it's a society that has advanced twenty years, and which now incorporates the wealth of multiple alien species."

"What? What do you mean, multiple alien species?"

"Over the last twenty years, several species of the Milky Way have integrated to an unprecedented degree. They've established a shared government as well as a shared military. Anyone who's able to subvert or corrupt that government, as Darkstream once did, would be the beneficiary of untold wealth and power."

Bronson scratched his cheek, creating a rasping sound. "What else has changed in the Milky Way?"

"Many things. You'll be surprised at the number of changes, almost all of them to our mutual advantage. The Darkstream board still lives, and so do you, Bronson. We have promised you will continue to rise, and now we can promise you revenge, too. Wouldn't you like some revenge for what those in the Milky Way did to you?"

Bronson squinted. "How do you know about that?"

"It's immaterial. You must answer now, Bronson. Do you accept my offer?"

"How do I know I won't just get arrested when I return to that galaxy? How can you assure me that I won't?"

"I said that you'll need some faith, did I not?"

After a long pause, Bronson said, "Okay. I'm in."

"Good. We will keep in contact." With that, the Progenitor returned to its enclosure, and the panel slid across of its own volition.

That was another first.

With that, Bronson left his office for the short walk to the CIC. He began barking orders the moment he arrived. "I need a wormhole opened right away, at a location we can viably defend for as long as it takes the civilian ships to pass through it. Tactical, collaborate with Nav to come up with the coordinates you judge will best accomplish that objective and then send them to the helm."

"Yes, sir," the Tactical and Nav officers said in unison.

"Coms, relay this message to the other battle group captains: they no longer have to worry about conservation of ordnance. Convey that I don't want them to have any Banshees left by the time we're on the other side of that wormhole, and instruct them to use whatever charge they have in their capacitors so that their lasers can supplement point defense systems in keeping the Ravagers at bay. This isn't about destroying enemy warships, necessarily, though that's certainly an acceptable outcome. Our main goal is to get every last one of our ships through that wormhole in one piece."

"The wormhole is open, sir," the helmsman reported.

"Excellent. Instruct the civilian captains to begin the exodus, and pass along the order for the entire battle group to form up in a rough half-sphere around the open end of the wormhole, with the other destroyers at the sphere's poles and us directly in front of it."

"Yes, sir."

That done, Bronson used his implant to send Price a private transmission.

Price studied him through narrowed eyes. "Yes, Bronson?"

"The wormhole's open, as requested. I'm arranging my warships to defend it now, and to defend the civilian ships passing through."

"They're not your warships, actually, Bronson. They're ours, now. Price out."

Bronson's nails bit into his palms, and his knuckles went white. But he stayed silent, and he bided his time. Just as he always had.

CHAPTER 49

That Was His Prayer

Roach wandered the Core of Valhalla Station, lost in memory. Buildings, green spaces, landmarks—almost everything reminded him of something that had happened here, or something that he'd made happen.

He passed the space elevator, charred and blasted open, though the smoke of battle had long since cleared.

This is it for me. I'm finished.

He felt no anger about the realization, toward Price or anyone else. He didn't feel angry at himself, who he knew deserved it most of all.

Instead, Roach felt deadened.

He might have left the station completely, gone in any direction he wanted—for a time. But the robots clearly had the taste of blood in their steel maws, and they would find him in the end. He was sure of that.

So he continued to wander, and eventually he heard a distant skittering, as though a thousand giant beetles approached across the great plaza.

At last, they drew into view: Ravagers, Gatherers, a few Amblers, and even more shapeshifting mechs—mirror images of himself.

They would tear him apart, so thoroughly that not even the alien mech would be able to resurrect him.

At least, that was his prayer.

No Matter What

"What do you see?" Jake asked the destroyer's sensor operator. The *Melvin* was the first ship through the wormhole, and moments after transitioning, the sensor operator's face had gone white.

"It's...gone."

"What's gone?" In the chaos of battle, Bronson hadn't told them where in the Milky Way he was opening the darkgate, and Jake hadn't asked. He'd been too busy watching the aged warships' desperate defense, wondering whether he would need to get in his mech to go outside and join the fight.

"We're in the Sol System. I can see Mars, Venus, and we're right next to Earth...they're all there, but there are supposed to be multiple colonies in the system, too. Those are all gone."

Jake's neck tensed, and he stared at the sensor data the officer was putting up on the viewscreen.

"I thought we won the war against the Ixa," Ash said from where she sat strapped into an observation chair, a couple over from Jake's. Her voice came out hoarse—she was still recovering from Roach's brutal attack outside Vanguard, but she'd wanted to be outside her mech for this, awake. Still, she'd grown quite thin, and her skin had acquired a frightful pallor. *She needs rest. She probably hasn't eaten since before the fighting on Valhalla.*

"Ma'am, we're getting a transmission request," the coms officer said to the captain.

"Put it through."

A man with a white-speckled beard appeared on the screen, squinting at them. "Who are you?"

"I'm Captain Vanessa Harding, Darkstream military. Who are you?"

"*Darkstream,*" the man repeated, his voice full of wonder. "You...you're back?"

"Some of us. Would you please identify yourself?"

"I'm Aden Shy, a project manager for the Earth Terraforming Initiative. No one's supposed to be in this system—not until the terraforming process is finished, which won't be for another couple centuries. And you're definitely not supposed to use a wormhole to get here, or anywhere, for that matter. The law is pretty clear on the use of dark tech. As a government employee, I'm afraid it's my duty to report you."

"That was the first instance of dark tech the company has used in twenty years," Captain Harding said, neglecting to mention the Majorana-infused decks included in everything Darkstream had put in space. "We had a pretty good reason for opening a wormhole. We were attacked by a species that wiped out most of our population. We're the only survivors, as far as we know. That same species, who identified themselves as the

Progenitors, claimed that *they* unleashed the Ixa on humanity, and now they plan to come for our species themselves."

Shy opened his mouth, then closed it again. Finally, he said, "This is well above my pay grade. I can send a message to my next higher-up, but from the sounds of it, you'll want the very highest levels of government."

"That would be ideal," Harding said. "What happened to the colonies of the Sol System, Mr. Shy?"

"Why, the Ixa wiped them out. Along with a lot of other systems. Wow." Shy gave his head a slight shake. "You have a lot of catching up to do, don't you?"

"It would seem so. How long will we have to wait before you hear from your superior?"

"Hard to say. The way things are these days, with the amount of bureaucracy we have, things can take a while. Having so many different species all wrapped up in the same government doesn't help matters too much. That said, this seems pretty important. I bet they'll want to send someone to speak to you right away." Shy cleared his throat. "What happened to you people, out there?"

"That's almost certainly going to be classified," Jake cut in. He unstrapped himself from his seat and made his way to between the Captain's chair and the CIC's main screen. "I'm Seaman Jake Price, and I command a team of heavy assault mechs. We've encountered multiple enemies outside the galaxy who are powerful enough that deploying mechs against them is likely our only chance of victory. We have the technology to build mechs, and we're going to need a lot more of them, but we're willing to share the schematics. We even have an unused mech we're willing to give you. Tell your superior to pass *that* up the chain."

Should get their attention.

Jake turned to find Ash smiling at him, looking satisfied. He nodded at her, returning the smile.

He had no idea what would come next, and the intel they had to share with the rest of humanity on the Progenitors was limited at best. But he did know that Oneiri Team was back, and no matter what confronted humanity next, they would be there to help stop it, together.

Acknowledgments

Thank you to Rex Bain and Jeff Rudolph for offering insightful editorial input and helping to make this book as strong as it could be.

Thank you to Tom Edwards for creating such stunning cover art.

Thank you to my family - your support means everything.

Thank you to Cecily, my heart.

Thank you to the people who read my stories, write reviews, and help spread the word. I couldn't do this without you.

About the Author

Scott Bartlett was born 1987 in St. John's, Newfoundland, and he has been writing since he was fifteen. He has received various awards for his fiction, including the H. R. (Bill) Percy Prize, the Lawrence Jackson Writers' Award, and the Percy Janes First Novel Award.

In 2013, Scott placed 2nd in Grain Magazine's Canada-wide short story competition and in 2015 he was shortlisted for the Cuffer Prize. His novel *Taking Stock* was also a semi-finalist in the 2014 Best Kindle Book Awards.

Scott mostly writes science fiction nowadays, though he's dabbled in other genres.

Visit scottplots.com to learn about Scott's other books.

Made in the USA
Las Vegas, NV
23 February 2021